Waiting for You

LEYA
LAYNE

Trigger Warnings

While this book is meant to be a cozy romance with spice, there are discussions of topics that could be triggering for readers. To be respectful to those who need warnings and those who see them as spoilers, I have placed the trigger warnings on my website. Scan this code to check the site.

Waiting for You was originally published in part within Falling for You in Cole County: A Cozy Romance Anthology in 2024.

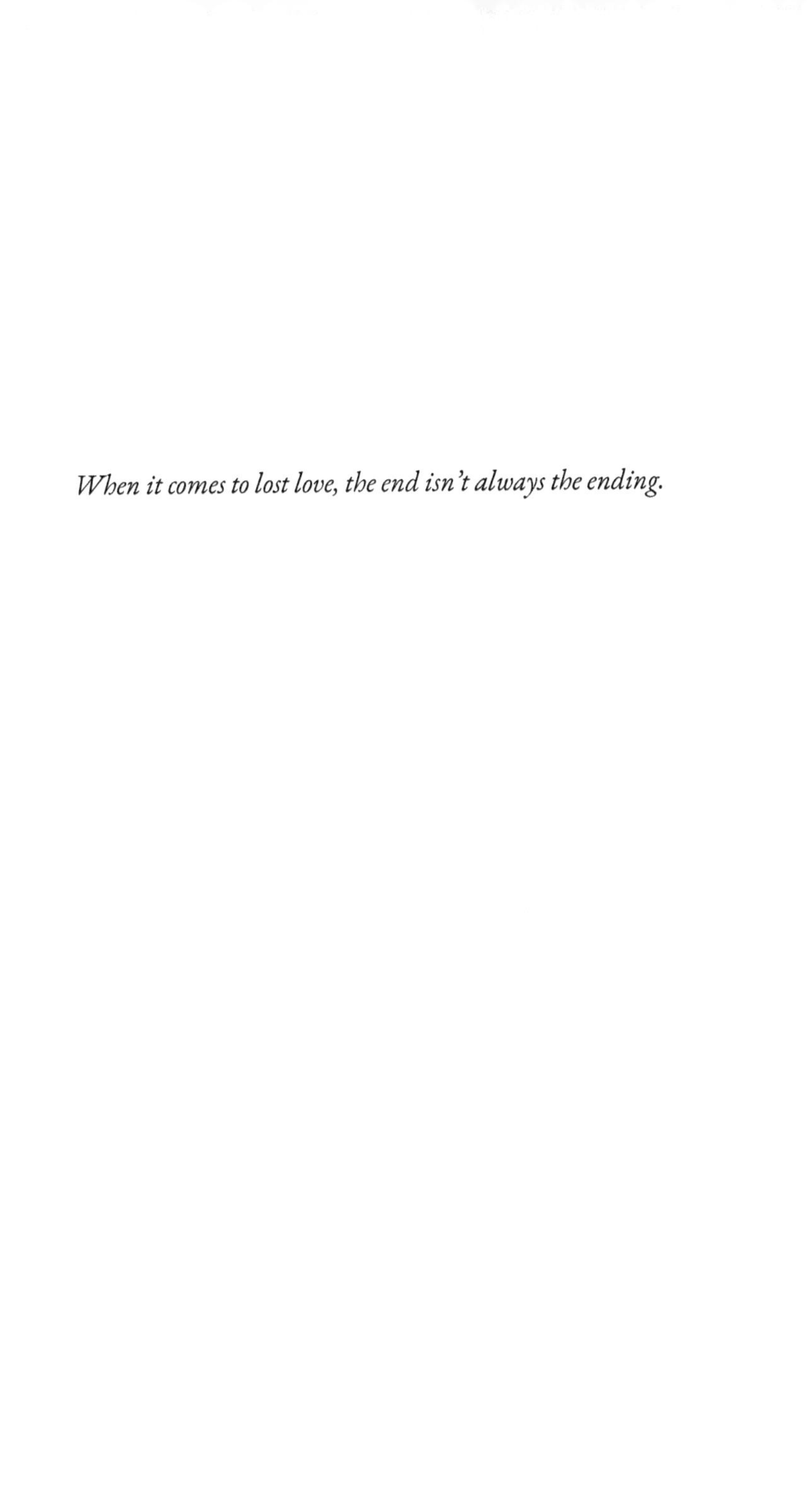

When it comes to lost love, the end isn't always the ending.

A NOTE FROM THE AUTHOR

Two years ago, my author besties, otherwise known as Roberts Row, had the crazy idea to do a cozy romance anthology series. They would be set in the same fictional county, and all the characters would attend the same seasonal event, whether or not they interacted with anyone else's characters. Thus, Cole County was born.

In the fall, our characters go to the Fall Festival. In the Winter, they attend the Lumberjack Showcase and get caught in a blizzard. In Spring, the rodeo comes to town. Summer brings it all full circle with the Summer Explosion.

We've loved this county and its inhabitants so much, new series have come from these characters and events. Old Man Wilber and Patches have become household names, and we had to bring you back one last time for the wedding of the century in our newest anthology Something Old, the first Magnolia Cove anthology, and the final installation of our collective Cole County offerings.

The creation of this world has been a labor of love, and there's other no group of authors I'd have wanted to build with. So thank you to Britton, Ashley, and Gracie for letting me in on this wild ride, and thank you to everyone who has bought, read, and gushed about these small-town, cozy romance stories.

I hope new readers come to love this world and these characters through these re-releases of Cole County Memories. I also hope those who've visited before appreciate the additions I've brought to these five stories. You deserve to have the full experience without word limits. I appreciate you! ~~Leya

WAITING FOR YOU

COLE COUNTY MEMORIES
BOOK ONE

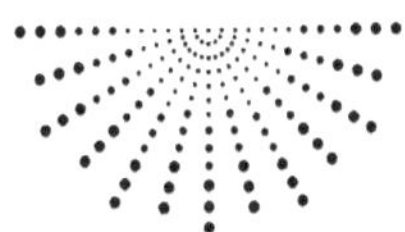

LEYA LAYNE

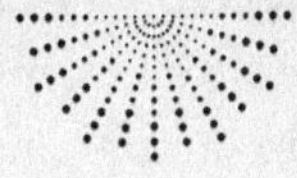

CHAPTER ONE

COMING HOME

Morgan

I pull onto the dirt entry at 2340 Canary Drive just before noon. The dilapidated wooden fence greets me with a crooked smile, its planks having cracked in the middle and fallen down into an awkward V. I sigh at the strange harbinger of misery and wallow in self-pity at having to move back to this backwoods town I thought to never see again. Memories of the best and yet roughest summers of my life under my grandmother's watchful eye flood through my mind.

My grandfather died years before I was born. After his death, my mother escaped to the city. Ha! What a city! Twenty years later, and the tallest building still has fewer than ten stories, and the total population sits at barely fifteen thousand. Still, there are parks and paved roads, so that's something, I guess. The important thing, though, is that Mother had truly escaped. Not once did she lay her head in this house. Instead, she would park in the large circular drive, help me get situated in her own childhood room, and be gone by dinner. She always claimed the need to get back for work as her reason for leaving so soon each trip, but I knew it was the fear of somehow getting stuck here that had her running twice a year.

"No more running for me," I say to the smiling fence while continuing the trip down memory lane on my way toward the house. Life had been difficult for my mother trying to raise me in Carruthersville, but she did everything she could to ensure we kept a roof over our heads and food on the table. Sometimes everything meant nights when I'd have to lock myself in the bedroom with music blasting through my headphones. Other times, it meant putting the chain on the door when Mother went to work at the bar at night. A shudder runs through me, and I put my foot on the gas, pushing forward. While those memories are all I have left, I can't allow them to damage the life I plan to build here.

Within moments, my car crests the hill at the end of the long, tree-lined driveway that's much shorter than I remember. As soon as I reach the clearing, the imposing house with its three stories looms just as large and steadfast as the woman who had owned it, though there's an air of disuse around the old place. The paint is faded and peeling from the double door entry, and my chest constricts at the sight. Though I'd hated the life-sucking pallor of this house as a child and young teen, I hadn't expected it to rot away. Standing here, I can hear my grandmother's voice scolding me for the neglect. "You can't expect to have nice things, Morgan, if you're not willing to work to maintain them." As an adult, the sting of that truth hits much harder than it ever had before.

"Oh well, let's get this over with." I close the car door and laugh when the lock chirps. Who in the hell is going to steal my car out here in the middle of nowhere? A ghost? Nah, the ghosts of my childhood live in my head. There's no way they want to live in this house. I don't even want to live in this house, but it's my one chance at stability. Losing my husband, my home, and both my mother and grandmother all in the same year has taken a toll on me financially, mentally, and emotionally. Thankfully, the leave of absence from my job came through, giving me the opportunity to come back to Canary Drive to try and regain some semblance of a life worth living. Bringing this house back to its former glory will hopefully give me purpose again and a chance to make amends for the resentment I've been harboring for the two women who shaped my life.

CHAPTER TWO

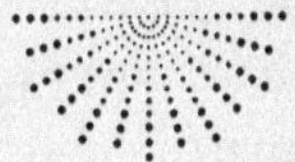

GHOSTS OF THE PAST

Morgan

Driving through Colliers Town proper provokes its own set of memories—Sunday mornings and Wednesday evening trips to the only church, as well as Saturday morning shopping trips to the market. Grandma Gretna would get her produce from the farm down the road, but all of the other items came from the town market. Sewing supplies and meat, cloth and cleansers. Though the town doesn't seem to have grown much, a lot has changed. There is a grocery store and a separate hardware store. There are also three gas stations along Main Street and four restaurants, including two pizza parlors and a Mexican *tienda* with photos of delicious looking plates of food in each window.

I pull into an on-street parking space directly in front of the hardware store at the same time my stomach growls. Thank goodness there are options for picking up dinner since I haven't eaten all day, and the kitchen isn't in any shape for cooking yet. There's much cleaning to be done before it will be usable.

Stepping onto the curb, I take in the quiet of the town. The main street in Carruthersville is never this empty, as there are always people around. While many people in the city lament the constant noise, I thrive on it. My thoughts don't get a chance to wander too much when there's a steady buzz of people. The sign on the hardware store says that it closes at 5pm. "Banking hours," I say aloud to the empty street, mimicking my grandmother's words whenever she'd mention the stores closing before dusk. A quick glance at my watch tells me I better stop reminiscing. It's already 4:30, which means I only have time to pick up the items I'll need for cleaning enough to be able to shower and sleep.

"We close in 30 minutes," a voice calls from the back of the store.

Thank goodness it's a woman working tonight, I think, my nerves calming a bit. I do not want to deal with a macho hardware guy trying to sell me things I don't need or attempting to offer his 'help.' I'd rather watch videos on the internet to learn everything I need than to deal with that.

"Thanks. I should be able to get everything I need in time."

"Let me know if you need any help."

With a smile on my lips, I make my way to the aisle carefully labeled cleaning with a handwritten sign. It's oddly satisfying to find that they aren't too modern here. It would totally seem out of place. I quickly locate buckets and gloves, bleach and cleanser, a broom and a mop. The fact that I couldn't find any cleaning supplies in the house was probably the weirdest part of the day. Grandma Gretna had been a neat freak, and the entire house smelled of bleach near daily. It's a surprise we hadn't been asphyxiated in our sleep.

"I think I found everything, at least for today," I say and start placing the items on the counter without looking at the clerk behind the register.

"Do I know you?"

Without missing a beat, I respond, "I don't think so. I'm moving into the old house out on Canary Drive."

"No, I mean, I know you."

Cautiously, I look the woman over. She's near my age, though she looks far less weary than I feel. Her brown curls don't quite match the light eyebrows, so she's likely a natural blonde. Though I try my best not to fixate on any one of the woman's features, her stare bores into me with an intensity that has me itching to run.

"Morgan? Morgan Humphries?"

"Oh wow," I say, "I haven't used that name in a very long time. It's Dartmouth, though that will be changing soon." As soon as the last part leaves my lips, I cringe. *What the hell, Morgan*, I chastise myself. *Nobody wants to hear that embarrassing truth.* Hopefully, the clerk doesn't pry any further, else I might just tell her all my damn secrets.

"Morgan Humphries, my word. I never thought I'd see you again. It's Joanna. Joanna Daniels."

"Joanna!" My voice raises two octaves at the revelation.

Joanna and I had been church buddies every summer. In fact, she had been my first friend when I started coming to Colliers Town. While other kids were allowed to run wild during the summer, Grandma Gretna rarely let me go anywhere. Occasionally, though, I was allowed to sit with Joanna's family and go to their house. Still, I could never sleep over because of Joanna's twin brother. My breath hitches as a name I haven't thought of in ages takes root in my mind—Jacob.

Jacob had always been there. When we were all ten, he put crickets down our dresses during service. Joanna and I got in trouble for squirming all over the place. His apology had been so authentic that I forgave him instantly, on one condition. He had to buy us ice cream at the pharmacy the following Sunday. Since he had already started working at the one service station in town, he had money to meet that demand. As we got older, his pranks became less frequent, and I became far more aware of him. He was my first crush and my first kiss. In fact, it was that kiss that signaled the end of my trips to Colliers Town each summer.

"Morgan, are you okay?" Joanna's voice breaks through the memories, exorcising the ghosts beginning to form.

"Yeah, sorry. It's just been a lot. Coming back here, I mean. So many memories." Not only am I rambling, but Joanna's expression says I'm not making much sense. I change the subject. "It's really good to see you, Joanna. You look good."

"You do too. All citified."

I make a show of looking down at my jeans, dusty from moving furniture and clambering through cobwebs. Sure, my blouse is a little more refined, but I won't be walking any runways any time soon as Miss Ex-Wife USA. Still, I can't help but giggle at the comment and the way Joanna leaned into her drawl on the last word.

"How's your family? Your parents? Jacob?" *Do I really want to know if he's still around?*

Sadness seeps into Joanna's expression and her words. "Ma passed away five years ago. Jake and I take care of Pa."

"I'm so sorry. I didn't know." I bite the inside of my cheek as thoughts of my mother and how hard the transition has been for me slink through my mind, ready to wrap around my heart again.

"How could you?" Joanna retorts sharply. "You left twenty years ago and never came back."

The words sting, but I can't argue with her. She's right. I left and never looked back. The same guilt that had begun to take hold while I rummaged through the house blooms. I've neglected so much over the years. In the house, the neglect of the past year is evident in the dust and rot, of course, but the disarray says that things had been neglected long before Grandma Gretna passed.

Before I can deep dive into self-loathing, Joanna breaks in with a question I don't know how to answer. "Why didn't you come back? I used to ask your grandma about you all the time, and she would never answer."

I let my eyes fall to the countertop where the nicks and stains broadcast the passing of time, but no amount of time will help in this situation. There simply isn't a good answer, at least not one I can say aloud. If Jacob hadn't confided in his sister about us being caught, I won't be the one to share the secret after all these years.

"I'm sorry, Joanna. I don't have a good reason, and I don't know why my grandmother did half the things she did."

"I thought we were friends."

Those words are all it takes to fray the last strand of my composure and have tears blazing a trail down my face. I didn't expect to see anyone I knew this soon. I'd hoped to not be recognized. It's all been too much, and my soul is still far too tender from the beating it had taken at the hands of my ex.

"Oh, honey." Joanna comes around the counter and wraps me in a tight hug. My arms go around Joanna's waist, grateful for the sympathetic support. The past few months have been hell.

"I'm so sorry, Joanna. So very sorry. We were friends. So, so sorry." Each apology comes out as a sob, and still Joanna holds me in silence. Somehow, much like when we were children, she knows exactly what I need emotionally. As the tears subside, and my breathing relaxes, I slowly release my old friend and grab her hands. "Can you ever forgive me?"

"I always had a soft spot for you. There is nothing I can't forgive. Your visits, and the time we spent together, provided some of my best memories of childhood."

The cuckoo clock announces the arrival of 5pm and time for the store to close. I let out a sigh of relief, but whether it is from Joanna's promise of forgiveness or the interruption of the moment, I'm not sure.

"C'mon, let's get this stuff rung up, so we can get out of here." I pull out my wallet, but Joanna shakes her head. "Just because you're from the city doesn't mean I'm gonna charge you for cleaning supplies. How does the old house look?"

I have no words. Joanna knew that mom and I had struggled to make ends meet. It was one of the things we talked about each summer when I arrived. Some years were better than others, but mostly, I showed up hungry and starving for affection. Grandma Gretna filled my belly, but it was Joanna who filled my soul.

"I can pay, J. I'm not the same girl I once was."

"Nonsense. My childhood best friend is back in town. Consider it my treat. Dinner too!"

She steps out from behind the counter without actually finalizing the sale.

"Wait, won't you get in trouble for not finishing my sale."

"Perks of being the owner," Joanna says with a wink.

I stand there staring at her back, dumbfounded. What else has changed around here?

CHAPTER THREE

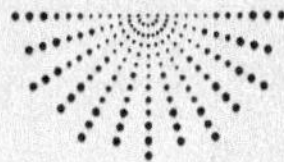

REMEMBER ME?

$\mathcal{M}$organ

Joanna and I put everything in my car, before making our way down Main Street on foot to the nearest pizza parlor. While we walk, she tells me about some of the changes around town, most of which I noticed on my way through, but I listen anyway. "As you can see, there still aren't lots of options around here, but things have gotten better. We have these two pizza parlors, a place for Mexican food, the gas station sells fried chicken, and there is a fast-food place opening next month." We step into the restaurant before she bumps her shoulder into mine with a laugh. "Soon you'll have all the comforts of home."

I chuckle along with her, relaxing into the conversation. The fact that she's willing to banter with me and spend time over dinner helps relieve the tension that has been constricting my chest. The restaurant is nearly empty, so we choose a booth in the front corner nearest the window but away from the door.

"Do you remember when they could've fit six of us in these booths?" Joanna asks unironically. "Now, I can barely squeeze my ass in one by myself."

My mouth opens as I stare at her. Joanna's maybe half my size, so her discomfort is unexpected. I, on the other hand, expect the booth to be tight; they're always tight. Still, I wouldn't mention it aloud in public. No need to draw attention to what's just a normal slice of life as a fat woman. After watching my mother make herself ill with starvation diets and weight-loss supplements, I decided long ago that I would simply live my life fat and happy. Unfortunately, I've only successfully managed one of those goals. I look at Joanna again and can't help but wonder if she's uncomfortable with her body?

"If you're not comfortable, we can move to a table," I offer.

Joanna shakes her head emphatically. "No, no. That's not necessary. I just wish that booth makers would recognize that not everyone is a size 0."

"Amen."

We both burst out laughing just as the young server comes to our table. It takes us a few seconds to settle down, so she hands us a couple menus and goes back to the counter. Not gonna lie, the menu is much more extensive than expected. Though Carruthersville is a very small city, most of the specifically named restaurants only carry those items. So, a pizza parlor like this one would only offer pizza and other food items made with pizza dough, maybe sub sandwiches. Here, however, the restaurant offers a little of everything, including cheeseburgers and fried seafood. When we place our order of two beers and a large pepperoni pizza, I muse aloud, "I'm gonna have to come back tomorrow and try something else. I might make it through the entire menu before the kitchen is in workable order again." She laughs, but I'm serious. The kitchen is trashed, and I'm not even sure if Grandma Gretna ever bothered to buy a microwave. Either way, it wouldn't be the first time I've eaten cold food.

"So, how is the house?" Joanna asks, cutting off my slow descent into painful memories. "No one here thought anyone would ever go back in it after your grandmother passed. Hell, rarely did anyone go in it while she was alive, especially not after you stopped coming around."

Okay, maybe I'm not meant to have a reprieve because that lingering guilt creeps up my back again. My grandmother had never been an overly friendly woman, but she had been social, especially on Sundays. So, the fact that the house stood mainly empty for years meant Grandma Gretna had spent all those years alone.

"No, no, no. Don't get that sad look on your face again, missy," Joanna admonishes. "Your grandmother did not live the life of a recluse, but she also did not invite guests to the house. That's not much different from when you used to come each summer."

I let out a sigh. She's right. My grandmother did not like people to come into her house. She would give a hundred reasons why it set a bad precedent to invite others into your space, but really, I think she didn't want questions that would come if others saw the pictures of my mother and grandfather that still lined the halls. She probably didn't want them to see the wooden highchair that still sits in the corner of the kitchen—the one that had been my mother's before it was mine. Gretna Humphries did not throw anything away, nor did she like change.

"The house is in such disarray, I can hardly make heads or tails. I don't know what happened, but I can't even get into the kitchen. The bedrooms are filthy, and forget about the bathrooms. Hence all the cleaning supplies."

"Would you like some help cleaning?"

I open my mouth to reject Joanna's offer, but instead of forming the words, it drops open further. The most handsome face I've ever seen has walked through the door. His hair is a sandy blond kept long enough on top to accentuate the thick waves while it's cropped neatly at the bottom. His smooth skin holds a beautiful natural tan that frames deep brown eyes I want to get lost in. His is a face I never expected to see again.

"Jacob."

Joanna turns around at the whispered name and summons her brother over with wave and a smile. I take him in, from the work boots on his feet to the jeans that fit him oh so right, to the paint-stained tee that pulls snug across his toned chest. He's barely changed, or maybe it's a matter of me having changed so much he seems caught in time.

"Hey, little brother."

"I'm going to ignore that for now since I need to get back to work." His voice is like worn leather, deep and smooth, and all I can do is sit there mesmerized. "You said you had something to show me," impatience colors his tone before he realizes I'm sitting here and turns his gaze on me. "Forgive my manners. My sister likes to make everything an emergency even when it's not. I'm Jake Daniels."

I smile up at him because how could I not when he's an easy six foot or so tall. My heart flutters when he smiles back, and Joanna giggles. I cut her a sideways glance, and Jacob looks back and forth between the two of us.

"What's going on?" he asks.

"She is what I had to show you. You really don't recognize her? It only took me thirty seconds." Joanna rattles on as if they had been in some contest to see who could guess my identity first. Good to see things between them haven't changed.

He ignores the taunts and turns his attention back to me, causing my cheeks to heat at the intensity of his stare. He looks back at his sister who's not letting him give up. Between the knitting of his brows and the tightness of his lips, as he examines my face, it's all I can do to not put him out of his misery.

"It's really okay if he doesn't remember me, J," I say, trying to cut through the stalemate, but Jacob cuts me off.

"Say my name."

"Huh?" His request is so unexpected, I swear I must've heard him wrong.

"Please say my name."

"Jacob."

He slides into the booth next to his sister and runs his fingers through his hair. Mine tingle with the urge to do the same. "Morgan Humphries," he says as if calling a ghost, like he can't believe I'm here, and I guess, in a way, he's right. I am a ghost "Wow. You're all grown up and back in Colliers Town. It's been what, twenty years?"

"About that, yes."

I think to tell him that no one calls me Humphries anymore since I've been married for almost ten of those years, but I don't want to answer any of the questions that would surely follow or feel their sympathy for my pathetic life. At any rate, I'll soon be Humphries again once the dust settles.

"Wow."

"You already said that, dodo," Joanna admonishes with a slap on his arm.

"You two haven't changed a bit," I say with a laugh.

He opens his mouth, but before anything comes out, the waitress shows up with our drinks.

"You joining them for lunch, sweetheart?" she asks Jacob, and my jaw clenches. I look away before anyone can read my expression.

"Nothing for me, Christine. I gotta get back to work."

When she walked away, he gets up from the booth, and I'm already dreading the loss of his presence "It's good seeing you again, Morgan. You gonna be around for a while?"

Fuck, how do I answer that question? Yes? I'm not sure? I hope so?

Thankfully, Joanna answers first. "She's cleaning up her grandmother's house. I'm gonna go over tomorrow after work. You should come help."

"That's okay. I'm sure he has plenty to do," I hedge. It isn't that I don't want him to come around. It's that I don't want his sister guilting him into helping like she used to do when we were kids. I also don't want him, or really anyone, seeing how terribly disheveled the house is. Grandma Gretna may have been a hard woman, but she doesn't deserve for her legacy to be reduced to the mess she left in death.

"If I get done early enough, I'll pop by," he says and then, just as quickly as he had arrived, he leaves.

I watch his retreating form until his head no longer shows through the windows. With a deep sigh, I turn my attention back to Joanna who sits there watching me with a smirk.

"You never could keep your eyes off of him."

I chuckle because she's not wrong and look toward the counter. Thankfully, the waitress approaches with our pizza.

CHAPTER FOUR

WISHING, WONDERING, WAITING

Jacob

Morgan Fucking Humphries. The sound of my name on her lips is like one of those fever dreams, something too good to be true. But here she is in front of me for the first time in twenty years. Twenty years of wishing, of wondering, of waiting.

"Wow. You're all grown up and back in Colliers Town. It's been what, twenty years?" I let the surprise seep into my voice. I'd honestly stopped believing I'd ever see her again.

A soft smile plays across her lips, but it's the sadness in her eyes that captures me. I guess I always imagined that she'd somehow found the happiness that had eluded her as a child. It was the story I told myself over and over as each summer came and went without her returning. To still see the pain reflected there has me itching to hold her, to force a laugh from her lips, to pull her hair like I had when we were kids. But we're not kids anymore, and the way every nerve in my body tingles with awareness, her sadness is not the only thing it remembers.

"About that, yes." The words are matter-of-fact, like she's

nothing more than a childhood acquaintance catching up and not my first love, my first kiss, my salvation, and my greatest torment.

"Wow."

"You already said that, dodo," Joanna says, slapping my arm playfully, but my attention is fully focused on Morgan.

"You two haven't changed a bit," she says with a laugh, and this time I let out a chuckle. If she only knew how much things have changed, the toll all these years have taken on both of us.

I go to tell her so, but don't get the chance when Christine interrupts our conversation. I clench my jaw at the intrusion and have to fight to release it before I can answer with a quick, "Nothing for me, Christine. I gotta get back to work." It's both true and an excuse. Christine and I have hooked up a couple times over the years, though nothing serious. Hopefully, Morgan sees the term of endearment as nothing more than the southern charm waitresses turn on for tips, because I don't want her getting the wrong idea. Suddenly, the air inside the restaurant is too thick, too hot.

I get up from the booth, trying to keep my movements smooth and controlled when I'm feeling anything but. "It's good seeing you again, Morgan. You gonna be around for a while?" She looks away, and my heart sinks. She can't be planning to leave already when she's just come back.

Thankfully, Joanna saves me from spiraling. "She's cleaning up her grandmother's house. I'm gonna go over tomorrow after work. You should come help." Air whooshes out of me from where I've been holding it. If Morgan's at her grandmother's house and needs help cleaning, she has to plan on staying, at least that's the hope my foolish heart conjures at the thought. I need to see her again, to talk to her, to apologize.

"That's okay," she says, looking at Joanna instead of me. "I'm sure he has plenty to do."

I almost laugh. She can't keep me away that easily, not when I know she needs help. Not when having her back in Colliers Town is like waking from a nightmare to find the sun has risen.

"If I get done early enough, I'll pop by," I say with a smile before turning to leave.

As soon as I get out the door, I take in a couple of deep breaths. My heart is thumping in my chest, and it's all I can do to calmly walk away. I want to turn and see if she's watching me like she used to when we were kids, before that day Gretna Humphries caught us behind the church, before she'd dragged Morgan away to never be seen again...until today.

"Until tomorrow," I say aloud to myself as I hop in my truck and pull away from the curb.

CHAPTER FIVE

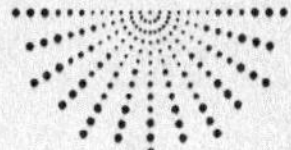

TACKLING THE UNEXPECTED

*M*organ

I wake with one question on my mind. Was this bed always so uncomfortable? My back aches, and my shoulders are tight. My hip might have been knocked out of alignment. If Joanna actually comes by today like she promised, I'm going to have to ask her the best way to get a new mattress or a new bed altogether. There's no way I can sleep like this for too many nights without completely falling apart. And I doubt I can just have one delivered from the internet out here in the middle of nowhere.

Normally, I prefer to sleep in a bit on Saturdays, but there's no point. I need to get out of this bed. Besides, all I'd managed to do last night was clean the hallway bathroom and take a shower. Else, I'd have had to pee in the dark green water that had been fermenting in the toilet all these years. This morning, the plan is to tackle emptying the kitchen. No doubt, there's long-expired food, and who knows what else in there. First, though, I have to pull out all the furniture.

By the time Joanna arrives, I've managed to make a path from the doorway in the hall to the door that leads to the back porch.

It's been so long since that door has been opened that the lock is rusted shut. I bang on it and the hinges with a hammer a few times to get it to open, so I can take some of the furniture out to the backyard rather than drag it through the house to the front. Unfortunately, that's not an option. There are holes where the old floor planks have rotted, and animals have burrowed their way onto the porch in winter. *The whole porch will have to go*, I think with a sigh. But that's a problem for another day.

Joanna pulls up the drive waving her hand out the window while I'm carrying out the old highchair. I can hear her singing along to some pop music channel. One of the things the three of us had in common all those years ago was that we were some of the only kids not into country music. Grandma Gretna didn't allow music other than old gospel tunes in the house, so the Daniels' house was the only place I got to listen to pop music. It makes me smile to see my friend's taste hasn't changed much.

"Hey there. I figured you hadn't yet gotten to the point you can cook in there, so I brought you lunch."

"You're a godsend, J."

"I know."

Joanna makes this statement with such animation that I can't help but laugh. She has always been overly dramatic. In a perfect world, she would have taken acting classes and been on stage in New York or in movies.

"Looks like you've gotten lots of work done already today. That must mean you don't need me."

"No, ma'am. You offered, and I'm taking you up on that offer. I found much more than I bargained for in there."

We eat out on the front porch. As soon as I take the first bite, ravenous hunger washes over me, and I realize I haven't eaten all day. Joanna really is a godsend.

After lunch, I give Joanna a tour of the house. Grandma Gretna had never allowed her in the house all those years ago, so it's all new. Her enthusiasm for the historical opulence of the place, even in its current state of disorder, helps assuage the fear that I might not be able to make something worthwhile of it. When we get to the kitchen, though, and Joanna looks out at the back porch, she whistles.

"Yeah, you're definitely going to need Jake's help with that. I may own the hardware store, but I am not Ms. Fixer Upper."

An uncomfortable chuckle bubbles from my throat. "Have you watched those shows?" I ask to distract us both from the sad reality of how much work really needs to be done.

"Girl, I watch all of them, and I still can't do shit with a hammer besides put up a picture frame."

I grab an empty box from where I'd dropped them on the floor and go back to emptying the cabinets that are finally accessible with all the big furniture out of the kitchen. I have so many questions for Joanna now that she's here, but I don't want to seem like I'm prying, so I settle on something that's hopefully innocuous.

"So, Jacob goes by Jake now?"

Instead of an answer, what follows is an ungodly shriek that makes me jump.

"What the hell? Are you alright?"

Joanna, who had taken on the job of cleaning out the appliances, stares into the open oven, her face pale. "There's a fucking dead mouse in the stove. There's a nest. Oh god, the smell."

She runs down the hall and out onto the porch, and I cover my nose before looking inside. Not for the first time today, I thank my lucky stars I had the good sense to buy a box of gloves with the cleaning supplies. Leaving Joanna to get herself together, I grab the broom and start sweeping the nest and dead mouse out of the stove and into a trash bag. After the sights and smells from the bathroom yesterday, this is nothing.

Heavy footsteps clomp down the hall, catching me off guard. Even in her sprint for fresh air, Joanna didn't walk that heavy. So, I tie the bag in my hands and turn around, ready for whatever, or really whoever, is coming.

"Hey, Morgana."

My breath catches as Jacob comes into the kitchen looking just as delicious as he had yesterday. Today, though, his hair is damp, like he showered before coming over.

"I haven't heard that name in forever," I say before turning away to hide the heat climbing into my cheeks.

He walks around until his eyes catch mine, and he gives me a sheepish smile. "My feelings might have been hurt if you had." The way he looks at me has butterflies flittering in my stomach, and I have to fight the urge to turn away from him again.

"If you came to help with the work, you probably wasted that shower. This is not for the church clothes crew."

His deep laugh reverberates through the room. "I don't wear jeans to church, Morgana. My ma taught be better than that."

"Jake no longer brings his ass to church," Joanna says, taunting her brother, and I can't help but wonder how she'd managed to sneak back inside without either of us noticing.

Jacob turns to her and holds one finger up to his lips. "Shhh, don't give away all my secrets."

"When did you start going by Jake instead of Jacob?" I repeat the question I'd asked Joanna immediately before she found the mouse. His response surprises me.

"When I came back home from bootcamp."

"Oh, you were in the military?"

He shakes his head, and I can't quite read the emotion on his face. "Not exactly. I enlisted and went to bootcamp. I didn't make it through."

"Oh." I don't know what else to say, or even any other questions to ask. There's a sadness in his voice, and there's no way I want to be the cause of anyone else drowning in the same melancholy that's flooded through me since I pulled into the driveway and saw this house for the first time in decades.

"Jake, we got the kitchen, but you might want to take a look at the back porch. It looks like it can use some of your special skills."

Something passes between the twins, and I get the sense Joanna is trying to distract her brother from the sadness too. I used to be able to read their silent conversations, but that ability is long gone, lost to the time I spent away from here. There's been so much lost over that time.

"Oh really?" His face lights up again, and he walks toward the door. "What's going on out here?" No sooner does the question leave his lips than he almost steps through one of the rotted boards. His hands catch the door frame, and he manages to pull himself back up to a standing position safely in the doorway. "Never mind, I found the problem."

Joanna and I both laugh, though my insides clench with embarrassment at the same time. "Still rushing headfirst into danger, huh, Jacob?"

He shrugs and then winks at me. "If I changed too much, you wouldn't have recognized me."

There go those flutters again. *Fuck me, Jacob Daniels is going to be such a distraction, a sexy, charismatic dream of a distraction.* With that thought, I go back to cleaning the cabinets before I do or say something stupid.

CHAPTER SIX

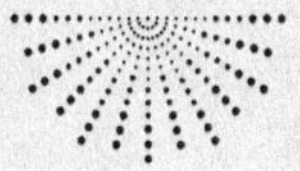

DISILLUSIONED

*M*organ

No matter how much I try to throw myself into the work, I remain unnaturally aware of Jacob being on the porch, just beyond the open door. It's the feeling of a storm coming when the pressure changes. Though Joanna is still in the room with me, the entirety of my consciousness pulls toward him like he's the moon and I'm his planet. It had been the same when we reached our teens. I always knew exactly where he was if he was anywhere in the vicinity, even more than his twin.

When he goes out to his truck to grab his tool belt, the house feels instantly empty, as if he's stolen all the air from the space. How does he still have this effect after twenty years? It's not like I'm still that teenager yearning for affection. I'm a 34-year-old woman with an entire life and marriage behind me, one where I managed to fall in and out of love in that time period. The fact that I had watched my mother hunt for love in the arms of many men and still pass utterly alone still aches. There is honestly no earthly reason why Jacob should even be on my radar.

"Morgan, what have you been up to all these years?" Joanna

asks from where she's hunched inside the refrigerator as if sensing the shift in my thoughts.

"I could ask you the same question," I shoot back with a laugh.

"You could, but I asked first, so you'll have to wait your turn."

We both laugh, and an overwhelming sense of gratitude for her still being here fills my spirit. I know we've not spent much time together yet, but it feels like we've picked up right where we left off. Our initial friendship had been built on sarcasm and a sense of belonging after all. *Maybe we had been sisters in another life*, I muse. As it is, though, we aren't sisters, and I'm here still lusting over her brother after all these years. Of course, I don't say any of that, much like I never told her how I felt back then, at least not about Jacob.

"Nothing to write home about really. I finished school and went to college for a couple years, but I didn't finish. I had gotten enough credits to let me work in a school as an assistant, so I did that for a few years. Then I met my husband."

bang "Ow!"

Jacob's yell penetrates through the kitchen, and I jump up to check on him. I find him lying on one of the few boards that isn't rotted through. His hammer is in the dirt under the porch, and blood is running down his face.

"Oh my god, Jacob, what did you do?"

I climb down into the hole he's opened by removing the rotten boards, so I can walk the couple of feet to him. He's staring up at the roof of the porch not moving or saying a word, and my heart stops.

"Jacob, are you okay? You're bleeding."

"He's fine," Joanna yells from the kitchen.

I cut my eyes back toward the door but make my way over to him.

"Talk to me. At least blink, damn it."

I lean closer to listen to his breathing. Since his eyes are open, he hasn't completely knocked himself out. He doesn't move, though. My foot touches his hammer as I move closer to his head, checking out the cut. Silently, I reach down and pick up the hammer. At the same time, I touch him lightly where there's a half-inch gash on his head. He winces so slightly I wonder if I haven't imagined it.

"Jacob Daniels," I whisper next to his ear, "if you don't answer me, I'm going to give you another gash on that hard head of yours."

His eyes roll toward me, and one side of his lips lifts into a half smile.

"You're a jerk, you know. I was genuinely worried that you had knocked yourself out."

"I almost did," he says faintly and tries to sit up.

He barely makes it to a seated position, lifting his shoulder from the board when his hand goes to his head, and his eyes roll back. I grab his shirt to keep him from tumbling backward. It takes a few more seconds before he grabs my arms and settles himself upright.

"I think I'm okay now."

"Just sit here for a minute and let me go find something to clean up that cut. Don't you move."

I head back through the kitchen and tell Joanna that he's cut his head but will be fine.

"I already told you he was fine. Damn drama king."

Joanna's words are terse, but I can tell that she's relaxed a bit. When cleaning the bathroom last night, I found an old first aid kit with some mercurochrome and bandaids. There might even be some peroxide in there. Without another thought, I run up the stairs and pull the items from under the sink. Joanna's watching her brother from the doorway when I return, but she goes back to work as soon as I drop down into the crawlspace.

"This is going to sting."

"How old is that shit?"

"I don't know, but how old are you that you hit your fool self in the head with a hammer? I'm betting we were young enough for it to have made sense when this stuff was bought." Somehow, I manage to keep a straight face, even when he wrinkles his nose.

"Did I hear right that you're married?"

I freeze. I hadn't planned to talk about my impending divorce with Jacob right now, maybe not ever. He, however, holds my gaze, and there's something in it that I can't quite decipher. I shake my head, and he lets out a breath.

"I'm days away from my divorce being final," I say quietly.

"I'm sorry, Morgana."

There it is again. That odd emotion flits across his face. His eyes are brighter than they had been, and though he seems genuinely sympathetic, I get the feeling he isn't exactly sad for me.

"Don't be sorry. It hadn't been a good marriage, at least not for a very long time."

"Are you happy it's over then?" Joanna asks from the doorway.

Do these two always listen in on others' conversations? *What am I thinking? Of course, they do.* They always have. One of the reasons I loved hanging out with them was because they knew so much about everyone and everything in the town. I never felt like I'd missed out on much because they filled me in almost as soon as I arrived each summer.

"I'd be lying if I said I wasn't devastated when Richard asked me to sign the papers. I was. But I was already reeling from my mother's death and the threat of losing my job because of dealing with all of that alone."

The backs of my eyes sting from that familiar burn, and I fight to maintain my composure. I already broke down once in front of Joanna yesterday. I refuse to let Richard's pettiness be the reason I do the same today but in front of them both.

"What about you two? Husbands? Wives? Partners? Dating? I will not be the only one in the hot seat."

The twins laugh and look at each other. Something passes between them, as it always has, and I fall into the old familiar pattern of waiting for them to decide who's going to go first and how much they're going to tell.

"You two haven't changed in the least. I mean, you've gotten a little taller, but you still do the same twin things I remember from way back."

Both of them narrow their eyes at me before Jacob smirks.

"No, don't you dare skirt around my question by asking me what I mean. You both know what I mean, and it won't get you out of answering."

Joanna goes first. "I was married young, right out of high school. He joined the Army and never came home, at least not whole."

I watch my old friend as she pauses her story and wonder if she's having difficulty continuing, but then she smiles.

"It was probably for the best. I mean, I hate to say it that way because I didn't wish him any ill-will at all, but we married real young. This is a small town, and though we've made progress, people still look down on divorce." Joanna stops again and looks at me with surprised eyes. "They won't judge you as harshly because you haven't been here in the community and church for a long time. They'd have shunned us, and we were both regretting the marriage even before he left. I've dated off and on since, but it is hard to find someone who I haven't known my whole life, especially not someone I haven't loathed for ninety percent of it. Maybe one day."

I laugh at her assessment of the guys in town and turned to Jacob. "And you?"

"Nope, never married. Dated, but nothing serious. I just haven't found the right girl."

"I hope you're not still looking for a girl at thirty-five, Jacob Daniels," I say with a playful wink.

He simply rolls his eyes and looks heavenward, causing me to chuckle.

"Anyone have any children?"

They both shake their heads, and I take a seat on the plank next to Jacob.

"Wow, what in the hell have we all been doing with our lives for the past twenty years?"

"I have a store," Joanna says with a smile.

"And I have a construction company," Jacob says from my side.

"And I have an old house that matches my life, full of shit and in disarray."

Jacob puts his arm around me and pulls me into a side hug.

"And you have us, just like it was all those years ago."

"On that note..." Joanna slaps the doorway. "I'm going to go grab us all something for dinner, and check on Pa. You two better get back to work, else it'll look like we accomplished nothing today."

"She still likes to be in charge, huh?" I ask, my voice barely above a whisper.

"You know it." His eyes shine in the setting sun that catches the porch before falling behind the tree line that surrounds the back yard.

I pull away from his arms and climb back up into the kitchen, determined to finish emptying and cleaning out the cabinets before dark fully takes over. I stop in the doorway and look back at Jacob.

"Thanks for being here."

He winks and goes back to pulling up rotted out boards.

CHAPTER SEVEN

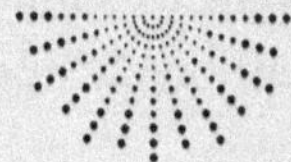

GLUTTON FOR PUNISHMENT

*J*acob

I can't believe she's fucking married. I shouldn't be surprised. She's the type of girl you marry—beautiful, funny, and attentive. That doesn't mean I don't want to pummel the guy who did it, who managed what I hadn't. It doesn't matter that we had been fourteen when she left. It doesn't matter that she never came back or called. None of that matters now that she's standing in front of me, tending to the wound my dumbass got because I hadn't even considered her having a life away from Colliers Town.

A hiss tears from my throat as she presses the mercurochrome to the scratch on my face. I want to tell her I'm fine and to keep that shit away from me, but the concern in her eyes holds me in place. My hands itch to reach up and touch her cheek, to see if her skin is still as soft as it had been the one time I got to touch that beautiful face. Instead, I ask the question that proves I'm a fucking glutton for punishment.

"Did I hear right that you're married?"

Sadness replaces the concern when she shakes her head, leaving me confused. Does the movement mean she isn't married or that she doesn't want to talk about it? I realize I've been holding my breath in anticipation and finally release it right as she says, so quietly I almost don't hear her, "I'm days away from my divorce being final."

Something akin to relief and sympathy curls in my chest, and I manage to say a simple, "I'm sorry, Morgana." I'm not sorry. Not in the least, but I don't want to sound too excited in case she's hurting. I would never intentionally hurt her. Not then. Not now. Not ever.

Before she can respond, though, my sister's voice echoes through the porch. "Are you happy it's over then?" I barely stifle a groan. Leave it to Joanna to ask the uncomfortable questions. Of course, I want to know the answer, but damn, the question has me cringing while Morgan's silence fills the space. When she finally answers, though, anger wells up inside me.

How could her husband, the man who'd had the privilege of being in her presence all these years, be so callous? How could he even consider letting her go? Grief ripples through Morgan as she shares how little the man had supported her through her mother's and grandmother's deaths. His selfishness fuels my anger. I want to put my arm around her, to pull her close and apologize for ever letting her go. Who cares that we were fourteen? I knew then that I loved her. Hell, she had bewitched me the first time she walked into the town church, quietly following behind her foreboding grandmother. The spell she cast over me is why I've always called her Morgana. She was an enchantress then with her sassy personality and sad eyes, and she's even more bewitching now.

I watch as she puts walls up around her emotions. The shift is so stark, I ache with being closed out. I may have tried to move on, but nothing ever felt as right as having her light cutting through the darkness. My mind wanders across the years and the emptiness in my heart no other girl has ever been able to fill. No one's even come close. Morgan's voice breaks through the jumbled mess of my thoughts as she asks what our lives have been like since we all last saw each other. Not for the first time, I wonder if she can read my mind.

Joanna and I look at each other, and I hope she can feel my reluctance. Though I've never told my sister everything that happened between Morgan and I, nor that I'm probably the reason she never came back, Joanna did know how I felt back then. I won't lie and say I'm sure how I feel right now, being near her after all this time, but there's no denying the pull between us. So, when I feel her eyes on me, I can't help but look up.

"Me? Nope, never married. Dated, but nothing serious. I just haven't found the right girl."

Her lips purse and a light pink tint floods into her cheeks before she responds with a snarky reminder that I'm too old to be looking for a girl. I put on a show of groaning and shaking my head. She's not wrong, though. I have been chasing after the feeling I'd gotten from the girl I knew twenty years ago, and I need to leave that pursuit in the past. Instead, I need to focus on getting to know the woman standing here now, and I plan to do just that as soon as I can get her alone.

CHAPTER EIGHT

FOR OLD TIME'S SAKE

*M*organ

Most of the kitchen, including the pantry is emptied and cleaned by the time Joanna returns with dinner. Jacob also manages to remove all the rotten and ruined materials, shovel out all the animal droppings, and seal off under the porch. When Joanna brings in an assortment of tacos, my stomach grumbles, once again reminding me that I've gone far too long without eating. The sun has begun to set behind the trees when we sit on the front porch. We eat in companionable silence, letting the work settle into our muscles as we enjoy the food. At least the silence lasts until I can't keep my thoughts to myself anymore.

"You know, I never thought I'd be back here in Colliers Town. If not for you two, I'd probably be hoping I'd fall through that back porch and impale myself on one of those boards." They both stare at me like I might go fling myself onto the back porch now, and I can't hold back a chuckle. "Anyway, that's my ridiculous way of saying, I'm so glad you two are still here because you make it feel like I can make this place home."

"It's good to have you back, Morgan," Joanna says. Her smile is punctuated with a yawn that's quickly followed by an apology for ruining the moment. "It's been a long day."

I open my mouth to tell her there's nothing to apologize for, but Jacob beats me to it. "Go home, sis. I'll help Morgana clean up this stuff and cover the furniture outside in case it rains. They're calling for storms in the next week."

I stand up and reach out to wrap Joanna in a hug. "Jacob's right. You've helped so much after working all day. I'll grab the tarps out of my car and call it a night myself."

Once everything outside is covered, Jacob and I make our way back into the house. He grabs his tool belt from the back porch and secures the door. I'm sitting on the stairs that lead to the second floor when he comes back in, my body and mind both wired and exhausted. He sets the tools at the foot of the stairs and sits next to me.

"Move your tall self up, so you're comfortable and not all scrunched up," I say without looking at him. The man's legs go up to my waist. There's no way he should be sitting this low.

He laughs and scoots up a couple of steps to stretch out his legs. We sit like that for who knows how long. My thoughts are all over the place, hyperaware of his nearness. In the name of self-preservation, I haven't thought of Jacob in almost 20 years, but ever since he entered that pizza parlor yesterday, I can't stop thinking about him. The fact that he's in my grandmother's house after, well, after 20 years has me spiraling with confusion and guilt.

"Why'd you never come back? Even as an adult, even after your grandmother's passing?"

I sigh. "Your sister asked me the same question. Are you going to guilt me with a 'I thought we were friends' too?"

"She didn't."

"You know she did."

He laughs. "You're right. That is totally something she would do right before giving you a hug and inviting you to lunch."

I elbow his leg and then join him in laughing at the ridiculousness of it all. It's so much better to laugh than to cry.

"I wouldn't want you to feel guilty about anything, Morgana. I had just hoped…"

When he doesn't finish his sentence, I turn to look up at him. "Hoped what?"

His dark brown eyes bore into mine with indecision. He breaks the connection and stares at the wall in front of the stairs. I sit there in silence giving him the time he needs. Lord knows I've often struggled for words lately.

"I had hoped for a chance to apologize."

I blink at him. My mouth opens to say something but then closes again as I try to process what he's saying. "Apologize for what?" I ask, my voice pitching higher.

"It was my fault you were sent home early. When you didn't come back the next summer, I knew that was my fault too. My ma even said your grandmother accused me of taking advantage of your innocence."

He doesn't look at me the entire time he spouts off those oh-so-wrong things. Grandma Gretna had berated me for being fast just like my mother and had called me a heathen, stopping just short of calling me a whore. She told me I was going to mess up Jacob's future prospects at a good woman and that she couldn't let my blood taint another good family.

"Leave it to my grandmother to punish us both with guilt."

His eyes snap back to me. "What do you mean?"

"She blamed me, my mother, and my tainted blood. She told me and my mother that I could not come back because I would ruin your prospects for a happy life."

Anger flashes through his eyes. I may have been struggling to recognize his other emotions after all these years, but this one is obvious. It doesn't take long before he's back to his normal even keel. That's one of the things I've always loved about him. Jacob isn't one for fits of emotion unless they're warranted.

One time, one of the boys from church called me a bastard and said my mother had been sent away because she was a whore who slept around. As soon as the first tear fell from my eye, Jacob jumped the kid. We were all young, so the boy's parents chalked it up to youthful impulsivity. I, however, had seen the change in Jacob's features. It wasn't long after that I started to notice much more about him.

"I waited for you," he says quietly after a few moments have passed. "Every year, I waited. When it became obvious you weren't coming back, I enlisted in the military." I gasp, both surprised at the revelation and grateful he hadn't suffered the same fate as Joanna's husband. "I got hurt during basic training. They didn't keep me, so I came back here."

I want to reach out and touch him, but I can't tell if that's what he needs or wants. So, I just listen. This is his story, not mine, even though I want to ask him how he was hurt and if it's something that still bothers him now.

"How's your head?" I ask instead.

It takes a moment before his eyes clear from that faraway look, and he focuses on me. "Hmm?" He puts his hand up to his forehead. "I hardly feel it at all."

"I guess the mercurochrome still works then," I say with a smile.

He smiles back and puts his hand on my shoulder. I cover it with one of my own.

"You were always a great listener, Morgana. You never held my uncertainties against me."

"I had plenty of my own, Jacob."

"Did you ever regret it?"

At first, I'm not sure what he's talking about. Did I regret all the uncertainties? Absolutely. When he stares at me intently, though, with the same look as when he said he'd waited for me to return, I know he's speaking of the kiss and everything that came after.

"The kiss? No, never. The aftermath that came from being caught? Yes. I lost everything good. A safe place to spend the summer where mother's visitors couldn't see or get to me. Friends. You." The last word is little more than a whisper, and when he doesn't move, his breath held, I follow through on the confession. "By the time I was old enough to bring myself back, I was afraid and embarrassed. I had been gone so many years. I didn't know if my grandmother would accept me into the house, and I didn't know if you were still here."

"So, you escaped in marriage." It's not a question, nor is it an accusation. It's a statement of fact.

"I got married," I agree. What I don't say is that I'd done so with the hope of being at least one step ahead of my mother. Charity Humphries had never gotten close to stability once she had me and left this house. Jacob simply nods, accepting the simplicity of my agreement.

"For what it's worth," he says quietly, "I wanted to come look for you. I went into Carruthersville with some friends once after graduation, but I didn't even know where to start looking. Then, when I'd healed after my discharge, Joanna talked me out of it. Her argument was that if you had wanted to be found, you would have at least written."

"She was angry with me." My statement, much like his about my marriage is matter-of-factly made. It's too late for pretending and regret. "Were you angry too, Jacob?"

"No. I was never angry, least of all with you."

"Thank you." A single tear slips from beneath my lashes, and he catches it with his hand on my cheek.

"Morgana?"

"Jacob."

He grabs my face with his other hand, and my breath quickens.

"Jacob," I say again as if he's an apparition that might disappear.

He slides down the steps until his face lines up with mine.
"No regrets, Morgana."
Our lips meet, though neither of us moves.

CHAPTER NINE

GASOLINE KISSES

Jacob

I hadn't meant to kiss her. Oh, I'd wanted to kiss her, but that wasn't my intention when I put my hands to each side of her face. Now, though, I have no intention of stopping. This girl I couldn't stop thinking about for years. This woman who still lights up the room. I'm lost to the dream that is having her here and in my arms.

Without letting our lips part, I reach around, threading my hands under her arms and pull her up against me. A little squeak leaves her lips, and I swallow it down. This is probably the weirdest position, but the feel of her weight on me is sublime, and I want more. My tongue slides along the seam of her lips, coaxing her to open fully. When she does, I nearly moan at the sensation.

"Morgan," I say between breaths, and she wraps her arms around my neck.

It's killing me that I don't know which room is hers, though it's probably a good thing I don't, else I'd be trying to carry her to it right about now. The way she's kissing me back hints at her wanting the same, but I don't want to be reading her wrong. She's not the one who's been pining away for twenty years. She's not the one who's been held in place by guilt and fear. She moved on. She built a life. She took a chance with someone else in some other place. Those thoughts should give me pause. They should probably make me angry. They should do anything besides make me want her more, but they don't. Instead, they remind me that I didn't try hard enough. I didn't do enough to find her. I didn't tell her grandmother and my parents the truth. Hell, I still haven't told my sister, my twin, the truth.

I break the kiss with a shake of my head, trying to stop the runaway thoughts. Morgan, my beautiful Morgana, pulls my face to look at her. Those beautiful brown eyes pierce straight into my soul, and I feel bare before her.

"No regrets." She throws my words back at me, and once again, I'm lost in the powerful spell of her. When she lifts her lips to mine, her tongue slipping in to tangle with mine, I stand and pull her with me.

"Where?" The single word is all I allow to come between our mouths before I reach down and hoist her up into my arms. She squeals, but I don't break the kiss, nor do I put her back down. She'll either wrap her legs around my hips, or they will dangle all the way up the stairs. I don't give a fuck which at this point. All it takes is the first step up, and she quickly wraps herself around me like a koala, holding on while our tongues continue to dance.

When we get to the top of the staircase, she reaches out a hand and turns the doorknob of the first room. I don't hesitate to turn in that direction and push it open. The room is small with little more than a standing wardrobe, dresser, desk, and twin-size bed. I almost chuckle aloud at the fact that I'll be making love to her for the first time on a bed more suitable for our fourteen-year-old bodies than those we've grown into. So much time lost.

I set Morgan down, letting our lips parts slightly. She looks up at me, her expression a mixture of desire and uncertainty. My lips graze her forehead and then the tip of her nose before I run my nose up her jaw, listening as she sucks in a breath.

"I'm sorry I don't have a better bed," she breathes out like she's been hiding from the reality.

"Oh, my little sorceress, I'd gladly lay myself on the floor at your feet and become your bed." Her eyes flash, lust widening her pupils with my confession. It's the truth. I would let her walk all over me and probably say thank you for the privilege.

"Jacob," she says on a breathy whisper, and I bring my mouth back to hers, fisting my hands in her hair.

This kiss is gasoline that ignites the fire within me I once believed forever extinguished. I don't want to just bury myself in this woman as has been my pattern over the years. I want to claim her and never let her go. My hands touch her everywhere, and she matches my passion, pulling at my clothes. Once we're both without shirts, I unclasp her bra and throw it across the room in a race to get my hands on her beautiful tits. They're full and heavy in my hands. When my calloused palms glide over her peaked nipples, she gasps. I waste no time in moving my mouth from her lips to her breasts licking around one taut nub before pulling it into my mouth.

"Jacob." My name is a plea, a prayer, and a promise. I bottle it all up and chug it down like life-giving water. Her moans are a symphony I want to hear over and over again. How have I been going through life without her? How have I been finding pleasure with others? How have I been breathing without her? In truth, I'm not sure I have.

After I've given sufficient attention to each of her breasts, I kiss my way up her chest, across her clavicle and up her neck, sucking at the sensitive flesh where her neck and shoulders meet. Then I capture her mouth again while walking her backwards to the bed. I follow her down across the mattress, her body dangling halfway off. When I stand to take in the sight of her, she tries to cover herself and sit up. A tiny shake of my head stops her. She licks her lips, and though the movement is more instinctual than teasing, my dick responds of its own accord, straining against the zipper of my jeans.

"You're so damn beautiful, Morgana. You put a spell on me years ago, and that magic has been the only thing holding my soul together."

I grab the waistband of her leggings and pull them off. Her skin is so fucking soft, and I want to bury my face between her legs. Their silkiness was made to glide across my cheeks. I want to take my time with her, love her right, but she sits up and reaches for my waistband, fumbling with the buttons to free my dick. She bites her lip when it springs free, and I nearly come undone from the sight of her salivating over me. There's no way I'll last if she pulls me into her mouth.

"Please tell me I can have you. Please," I beg. Everything in her expression and the way her body moves says that she's definitely a willing participant, but I need to hear that she wants me.

"Jacob Daniels, I need you. I want you. Let's not waste any more time."

Her words are all it takes for me to strip the rest of the way naked and climb over her beautifully soft body. She's scooted fully onto the bed, so I can climb between her legs, and fuck if I'm not about to blow like a fucking teenager before I even get inside of her.

With gritted teeth I place myself at her entrance and slowly push in. I don't want to hurt her since I haven't been able to fully prepare her for me, but she's already hot and wet. Still, I hold back from fully seating myself on the first thrust. My plan is to work myself back and forth, to let her get acclimated. She has other plans.

Before I realize what she's doing, she grabs my hips and pulls me into her while lifting herself up to meet me, and fuck if I don't slide home. We both moan like something has fallen into place, a lock finding its key. I lean down to kiss her lips, and she opens for me, pulling my tongue into her mouth the same way her heels pull my hips forward, sliding my dick into her sweet, sweet pussy every time I pull outward. When it becomes obvious she's not wanting slow lovemaking, I sit up on my knees and pull her hips upward, wrapping her legs around me. She looks up at me with fire in her eyes, and I set a pace to match that intensity.

There aren't words for how good she feels or how right this moment feels. She matches me with each thrust, her moans the soundtrack of us. "God, baby, you feel so damn good, so right, so perfect, like you were made for me."

"Jacob. Jacob. Jacob." My name chanted from her lips is all it takes to have me pounding in and out of her. My jaw clenches as I feel her walls begin to tighten around me. I will not come before she does.

"Fuck, Morgana, the way you're squeezing me." I slide a hand between us and press my thumb against her clit, rubbing small circles around it. Her breaths pick up until she's all but panting. She tries to cover her face with her arm. "Don't hide from me, beautiful sorceress, let me see you come undone."

"Jacob, I..."

I watch her face to see her expression shift from focus to surprise and then wonder as her walls begin to pulse around my dick, moans falling from her lips. "That's it. So, fucking good." It isn't until I cry out, my own release spilling into her, that I realize we didn't talk about birth control. Fucking reckless. I've always been so damn reckless for this girl.

I look deep into her eyes where they watch me with wonder. "Shit, baby, we didn't..." I cut off, fighting for the right words.

"I have an IUD," she says before I can say anything else, and I breathe out, willing my heart rate to calm.

"I'm clean, so you don't have to worry about that," I ramble out before pulling my half-staff dick from her pussy and standing from the bed. She so fucking beautiful like this, her cheeks flushed and her body surprisingly relaxed. I wish I could read her mind right now, but I can't, so I run out of the room to the bathroom with a quick, "I'll be right back."

It takes me a little longer to return to the room than I expected. "Sorry. I couldn't find the bathroom." She chuckles a little. The statement is true. I did have a hard time finding the bathroom since I'd never before been in this house, and all the doors were closed. It's only half true, though, because I also stood in front of the bathroom mirror berating myself for all the things I did wrong tonight, and all the reasons she'll likely be gone by the time I come back tomorrow.

Rather than hand her the towel, I kneel at the side of the bed and wipe her down, cleaning the remnants of our releases from between her legs. She watches me with what looks like curiosity, which piques my own. Has she never been cleaned up after sex? The words stick on my tongue when she stands from the bed. I stand too and grab my jeans from the floor, ready to let her get some sleep, but afraid to leave, afraid she'll leave right after I do.

Morgan stops in the doorway, her head tilted to the side. "I'll be right back. I just have to pee." I give her a soft smile. Her eyes drift down to where I'm holding my waistband, ready to put them back on. "You're not leaving, are you?"

"I, um, I wasn't sure...I didn't know if..." She stands there patiently while I stammer through the words that just won't come. Finally, I settle on something easy. "Not if you don't want me to."

"Good. I'll be right back," she says before disappearing down the hall.

I look toward the tiny bed, not sure how we'll fit comfortably but not caring one bit. I let the pants fall from my hands and turn down the covers.

CHAPTER TEN

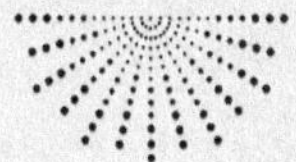

BROKEN AND WOUNDED

$\mathcal{M}$organ

I wake cocooned in warmth and comfort the likes of which I haven't known in years. It takes minutes before my brain fully recognizes the arm around my hip and the body pressed against my back, not to mention the fact we're both naked. Last night, there had been no thinking, no pretense, no fear, just a sense of home.

Jacob kisses my shoulder and runs his hand across my waist. The butterflies start in the pit of my stomach and work their way down.

"Good morning, Morgana. How do you feel?"

I turn onto my back in this bed that's far too small for us to sleep side-by-side comfortably and looked up into his eyes. He's still as beautiful as I remember him being at fourteen. Only now, I know what it means to want him in a way I couldn't have imagined when we'd had our first kiss. His smile is a balm on the feelings of loss from the past twenty years.

The light of day, though, reminds me of things left undone and words left unsaid. I wouldn't regret this time we had together, but I'm not ready to just pick up and move forward as if twenty years haven't passed. That thought, though, flees from my mind, as his mouth finds my breast and his hand slides between my legs.

My back arches, and I spread my thighs, giving him better access. Last night was fast and furious, as if afraid someone would once again step between us. This morning, however, Jacob takes his time, savoring my body, and when he trails kisses down to my sex, I don't want him to stop.

"Jacob."

He looks up into my eyes as he settles himself between my legs. He reaches around my thigh and opens me to him. Only then does he look down at my sex on full display. A smile plays across his lips before he opens his mouth on me, sucking and licking, his tongue doing glorious things to my body.

"Please."

He has me so close to the edge, I can hardly keep my thoughts straight. I grab at his head and grind into his face, chasing my elusive orgasm. While Jacob had managed to pry one from my body last night, it's never been easy for me. In the ten years we were married, Richard had only managed it a handful of times. Still, I had hoped it would just happen with Jacob, but my brain just won't connect, or rather disconnect, from my arousal. Not when he's touching me so intimately, the sensations penetrating far deeper than the surface of my body.

"Jacob, I need you."

"I'm right here, Morgana," he says, lifting his mouth from my clit for a moment before diving back in. Rather than drowning in the sensations, frustration pulls me further away. I just want it to be over, and if I learned anything from my mother and my husband, getting the man off is the sure-fire way to end the situation. It doesn't take long before Jacob lifts his head again with a quizzical look.

"What's wrong?"

I try to hold onto the frustration and the plan to get him off rather than address the elephant in the room. I try, but tears give the secret away. Jacob climbs back up my body until we're nose to nose.

"If that wasn't good for you, Morgana, tell me what you need. What will make you feel good?"

Tears fall in earnest, and the cloak of melancholy wraps around me again. The moment of peace I'd felt upon waking in Jacob's arms wasn't meant to last. I hadn't earned it. *You can't expect to have nice things, Morgan, if you don't work for them.* My grandmother's words come to the forefront of my mind, and I close my eyes against the guilt.

"I don't deserve any of this. I've not earned it, and I can't just pretend like the past twenty years haven't happened."

Jacob sits up. "What are you saying, Morgana?"

"I'm saying I'm not that girl you kissed twenty years ago. She was too broken to have survived all these years. Can you honestly say you're that same boy? That you've remained unchanged and unscathed by the years?"

He looks at me for a long while before agreeing that he has changed.

"After waiting for you for so long, I guess I just wanted the magical happy ending."

I cup his cheek. "I have no magic, Jacob. I've not thought myself a sorceress in decades."

"And last night?"

"Last night was a wish, like blowing on a dandelion. It was to help heal a wound that neither of us should have had, but it doesn't change the fact that we don't know each other as we are now."

He gets up from the bed and begins pulling on his jeans. Once he's found his clothes, he gathers mine and hands them to me. I slide into them and slip on my shoes.

When we get to the bottom of the stairs, he turns back to face me and sticks out his hand. Taken by surprise, I simply look between his eyes and his outstretched hand. When I finally offer my own, he grasps it tight and shakes it as if we're just meeting for the first time.

"Good morning, Miss. My name is Jake."

I let the air out through my nose and then smile warmly. "I'm Morgan. It's very nice to meet you."

"Likewise." Without letting my hand go, he turns my palm over and kisses the inside of my wrist. "Can I let you in on a little secret, Miss Morgan?" With one eyebrow raised, I nod. "This may seem a bit forward, but one day, I'm gonna marry you."

My breath catches, and my eyes go wide. Jake lets go of my hand and turns on his heel. He doesn't even look back when he exits the front door into the rain. As soon as the door latches, I slide down to sit on the stairs just like I had been when he found me the night before. This time, though, he's left me alone to consider his final words. No threats. No guilt. No regrets. Just a promise for the future. Do I dare look ahead?

CHAPTER ELEVEN

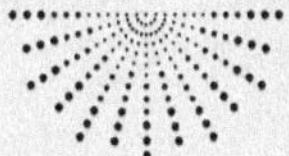

TIME STANDS STILL

$\mathcal{M}$organ

The days pass in a flurry of activity. I scrub and paint and sand furniture to prepare for refinishing. I might not have money to buy all new pieces, but with a little creativity, I can rework Grandma Gretna's heavy wooden furniture into something more modern and brighter. Lord knows this house can use some brightening up.

Joanna stops by every evening after closing the hardware store to help for about an hour. She is a godsend, picking up our friendship as if there hadn't been a major break. She texts each afternoon to see if there's anything I need for the evening or the next day, and she brings dinner with a little extra to last through the next afternoon's lunch. I haven't had to step foot back into downtown Colliers Town since the day I arrived.

Though Jacob hasn't been around or contacted me himself, he sends word via Joanna that he'll be here this weekend to finish the back porch and do any other major projects I need done. I shouldn't be excited by the prospect after what happened between us, but I am. Supposedly, he put someone else in charge of the jobs his company has scheduled for Saturday afternoon. I smile for

Joanna's sake, trying not to let on about the intimate night and awkward morning Jacob and I shared.

"Jake texts me at least 10 times a day asking about you, if you need anything, and if things are going well here at the house. Did y'all not exchange numbers?"

I nearly choke on the bite of meatball sandwich I'd just taken. Joanna looks at me expectantly. Shit, Jacob must not have told her anything either.

"No. We worked and chatted before he went home, but neither of us thought about our cell phones. Honestly, I'm surprised I get a signal out here."

Joanna snorts. "We are not that backwoods anymore, Morgan, sheesh."

"Well, you do still only have one major road and a small mom and pop grocery store."

"We, my friend. You're back home now. Besides, we also have a hardware store owned by the most awesome woman in town."

I respond with an exaggerated guffaw, and Joanna slaps her hand to her chest as if offended before doubling over in laughter as well. I absentmindedly pick up my sandwich before pausing to muse aloud. "I'm going to owe you my second-born by the time I get fully settled and start working again."

Joanna shakes her head emphatically, though there's a smile on her lips. "In my experience, the first-born is the better of the two in all ways."

"I'm telling your brother you said that," I say with a giggle.

Though I'm grateful for the renewed friendship with Joanna, I can't help but feel a bit sad that rekindling the same way with Jacob hasn't been as easy. Of course, our relationships are distinct, but that fact doesn't make it bother me any less. Before Joanna can read the shift in moods, I stuff the last few bites of dinner in my mouth.

Once we've finished our sandwiches and gathered the trash into the kitchen can, I grab the cleaning supplies and get back to work. There's still so much to be done just to make the house truly livable. That doesn't include all the upgrades and structural changes I'd like to do, including knocking out a couple walls that close everything off like individual tombs.

The center of the house is so dark unless the lights are kept on. There are no windows in the front door or in the hallways on either of the upstairs floors. The only way to get light is from the kitchen or to leave every door open to every room, so the sun can shine through from the outer walls.

"I'd like to invite you guys for dinner this weekend," I say as we enter the formal dining room. My grandmother never used this room, at least not when I was here. The room is huge with dark wood paneling and a large fireplace at one end. I've already taken down the heavy drapes to wash them, but I'm hoping to change them out for something airier and more sheer, something that might tame the imposing room.

"You don't have to do that. Save your money until you can get fully settled."

Tears burn the backs of my eyes at the understanding and empathy my friend has always shown. No one else has ever tried to understand my struggles and stand with me through them. No one else since Joanna and Jacob. A knot forms in my throat, and it takes a moment to swallow it down before I can respond.

"I want to. I haven't cooked in what feels like ages. Now that the kitchen is once again usable, and the dining room is just about ready too, I feel the urge to cook. Please don't make me cook for just myself."

Joanna looks into my eyes and then grabs her phone. Within seconds she has the thin device to her ear and is saying, "Don't schedule anything for Saturday night. We have dinner plans. Don't worry about it, just be available. Okay. Bye." Before saying another word, Joanna reaches down into the bucket of warm sudsy water and squeezes out a rag to wipe down the walls for painting. "Jake will be here too."

CHAPTER TWELVE

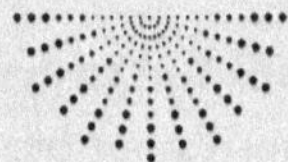

GLIMPSES OF HOPE

Jacob

Dinner plans? I think to myself. We're not the kind of people who have dinner plans. We don't do lunch, and we don't have tea. That's some city shit.

Morgana. Her name runs through my mind like a freight train. She has to be behind the sudden "plans." I haven't talked to her since the morning I slipped up and basically proposed to the woman right after she said she wasn't ready to pick up where we'd left off. I couldn't help it. The woman reappeared out of nowhere after twenty years, and my brain glitched. There's really nothing else to it. It has to be a glitch in the same way me asking Joanna about her every hour or so is.

Honestly, my sister should be happy I'm not texting every time I think of Morgan. I mean, I've thought about her often over the years, but those thoughts were nothing more than remnants of dreams long gone. Having her here in town, though, that's like being given a second chance at life, at happiness.

"Watch out!" a voice calls from behind me. I whip around just in time to duck before one of the trusses takes me out. I look up into the horrified face of our crane operator and lift a hand. 'I'm alright,' I mouth to him while trying to get my heart back under control. That could've gone so damn wrong.

"You alright, boss?" my foreman and good friend, Trevor, asks. He's sidled up next to where I've moved out of the crane's trajectory.

"Yeah, it missed me."

"That's not what I mean. You've never been distracted on a site before, but damn if your head's not been elsewhere this week, and now your head was just about on the ground."

I chuckle, but he's right. My head hasn't been here. It's been between Morgan's thighs, stuck on the fact that she let me take her, taste her, but not savor her. I keep replaying that kiss on the stairs, the moment I slid into her, and that first time my tongue dipped between her legs.

"Earth to Jake. Come in, Jake." Trevor's shaking his head when I finally focus on him again. "You've got it bad, man. So, what's her name?"

"You don't know what you're talking about," I say with as much vehemence as I can muster. It's not much, and we both know it. I can see the tip of Trevor's bullshit meter registering the need for a shovel and some hip boots.

"Hey, you don't have to tell me, but what you do have to do is get the hell off my site if you can't keep your mind on what we're doing here. You might be the boss, but it's my job to keep everyone safe, and I sure as hell don't want to have to pay for Cody's psychiatrist bill when he knocks your head off your shoulders with one of them trusses."

"Shit," I say, putting my hands in my pockets. "That obvious, huh?"

"Yeah." He clasps a hand on my shoulder, and I feel the weight of his concern.

Trevor and I have worked together a long time and been

friends even longer. Not once has he told me to go home from a site, not even when I was sick or exhausted. Hell, he never stopped me from working myself to death after my mother passed and Pa lost himself to grief.

"Let me go check on Pa, maybe take him to lunch."

He gives me a half smile. "Sounds like a great idea."

"Smart ass!" I throw over my shoulder as I walk away.

"So, what is her name?" he yells at my back with a deep laugh.

"Morgan," I say before climbing into my truck. I turn the key in the ignition and watch his face for the moment of recognition. As soon as his eyes go wide, and he opens his mouth to say something else, I throw the truck in drive and take off.

*J*acob

"Pa!" I yell when I enter the house.

Though I've been back home the past couple years to relieve Joanna from full responsibility for our father, it still feels weird to walk through the door without calling out a greeting. Pa is pretty laid back, but he still owns a shotgun and isn't afraid to use it. Ma would just yell at us for being rude. Thinking about Ma has me stumbling. It's been years, and I still can't believe she's gone most days.

"Where are ya, old man?" I say aloud, mostly to myself.

"Sitting right here."

His deep baritone booms from behind me to my left where I hadn't bothered to look when I came into the house, and I almost fall into the recliner on my right. Heart racing, and irritation coursing through my veins, I turn to where he's sitting on the couch. I haven't seen my father sitting in this room in years. Normally, he's in the kitchen nursing a cup of coffee long gone cold.

"Jesus, you just scared the crap out of me."

"Heh," is all he says, but there's a glint in his eye telling me there's something more on his mind.

Narrowing my eyes, I sit on the recliner with my feet firmly planted on the floor. We look at each other for several minutes before I can't take the silence anymore.

"What's going on, Pa?"

He runs his tongue along the outside of his teeth as if something's stuck there, and then he gives me a knowing smile. The only thing is, I have no idea what he thinks he knows.

"Do I need to call Joanna and have her come home? You're acting kinda funny. Well, funnier than usual." I try to keep my tone light. Ever since Ma passed, we never know what we're gonna get from him. Some days, he just sits in the same spot for hours at a time without moving. On those days, it's a chore just to get him to eat, and he won't talk at all. Other days, he wanders the land, like he's searching for something. Those are the days that worry me the most. Anything could happen to him out in the fields or the woods on the edge of our family's farmland. Today, though, his face is more animated than I've seen in ages.

"Funny you should mention your sister." He looks at me expectantly, and I can't do anything more than blink at him. "She told me that a little bird flew back into town after many years." Again, his eyes bore into mine. I'm not sure what he's waiting for me to say.

"Oh, yeah, her old friend, Morgan, came back to clean up the old Humphries house. I'm surprised you remember her. I almost didn't when I saw her."

His smile brightens, and a knot starts to form in my stomach. What is happening?

"Didn't recognize her, huh? She change a lot?"

My brows furrow. "It's been twenty years, but I was, honestly, too focused on trying to figure out why Joanna had called me to the pizza parlor." I chuckle at the memory, and his brow lifts.

"When she told me she had something important to show me, I never expected it to be a person."

"That doesn't answer the question."

"Fine," I say with a sigh. "I didn't recognize her until she spoke. Then I asked her to say my name." I look up and catch my father's eyes, clear in a way they haven't been in a long while, before I add, "Hearing my name on her lips took me back all those years. It was like coming home, Pa. I'm not really sure I can explain it."

"Sounds to me like you explained it just right. You had a thing for that girl years ago, and it sounds like that thing is still there."

I look down at my boots. It does not seem to matter how old I get, I don't want to talk about women with my father. "You seem to be in a good mood today," I say, hoping to change the subject. His look tells me he knows that I'm trying to distract him.

"You never were that good at hiding your feelings, son. All I've ever wanted was for my children to be happy. I guess I haven't done a very good job conveying that message." He looks at me, and I'm not sure if he wants me to argue that he has it wrong or agree. The truth is, he's made the message clear, but he's not made it easy to achieve. That's not something I want to say, though, especially not on a day he's actually in good spirits. "Well, anyway, I was glad to hear the excitement in your sister's voice when she told me Morgan was back, and I'm glad to see you're also happy about her return."

"I am happy, she's back, Pa. We're helping her out at the old house. She's turning it into a bed and breakfast. I'd be glad to have the help if you're ever feeling up to it."

His demeanor changes at my offer. The smile he'd been wearing drops, and his shoulders droop.

"No pressure, Pa. Just thought you might like to come out and see how the old house is coming along. I'm not sure if you'd ever been inside it. I know I hadn't until Joanna talked Morgan into letting us come help renovate and clean. If you're not up to it, it's alright."

Pa turns his head to look out the window, and I know I've lost him. The light that had shone in his eyes has dimmed again. As I watch him fade back into the oblivion, my eyes burn, and I head into the kitchen to make us some dinner.

CHAPTER THIRTEEN

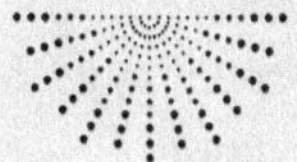

CALM IN THE STORM

*M*organ

Saturday morning is a whirlwind. I wake up early, sweep and mop the rooms we'll be using, and run to the grocery store for the ingredients I need for dinner. Though I have many years of experience working in a kitchen, the money just isn't here to splurge on anything too fancy, so baked ziti with homemade meatballs and garlic bread, it is. Simple, tasty, and easy cleanup.

I love to bake my meatballs and steep them in homemade sauce, so I make sure to put them on before lunch. The ziti is easy enough to mix and put in a pan an hour before Jacob and Joanna are supposed to get here. I want everything ready to go in the oven as soon as Joanna texts to say they're on the way. Once I have everything prepped, I make my way into the dining room.

I set the table for the three of us, complete with wine glasses I found in a box at the bottom of the hall closet. Maybe my grandparents had parties in the house years ago because there's no way Grandma Gretna used those glasses. Perhaps it was my birth, or maybe my grandfather's passing, that had been the reason the parties stopped.

Never mind that, I tell myself. There's no time to dwell on the past, although I have discovered some wonderful finds while digging through closets in each of the bedrooms. For example, in the closet across the hall from my old room, the room with the world's most uncomfortable bed, I found a stash of board games. There's an ancient version of Monopoly, an original Game of Life, and Scrabble, amongst many others. The multi-player games currently sit on the dining room table. Maybe my friends will want to play a game or two after dinner.

The rest of the afternoon is spent scrubbing the top-floor bathroom. Though I'm the only one in the house, something about making sure all of the bathrooms are clean and in working condition is important to me. I tackled the main-floor water closet the day after I arrived, the day after I'd had to scrub and plunge and dig through the muck of the second-floor bathroom. The only room I haven't touched, haven't even opened the door to yet is my grandmother's.

Gretna Humphries always had a strong lock on her bedroom door that she kept closed tight whenever she wasn't inside. She never left the door open, even if she was in there. In fact, I can't remember ever hearing her leave the room in the middle of the night or early morning to use the bathroom on that floor. Though it hadn't bothered me as a child, curiosity sparks at the thought. The main floor only has a water closet, not a full bathroom. Is it possible there's an ensuite behind that door?

I grab the box of all the loose keys I've found around the house, as well as the ones that had been sent to my mom when Grandma Gretna passed. Even without the woman's looming presence, standing in front of her bedroom door feels much like standing outside the principal's office. Not to mention, I have no idea which key, if any, will open the damn thing. Looking down at the collection in my hands, I prepare myself to try them all.

I pull out the sets of keys Grandma Gretna always carried on her person first. It only makes sense that she would have the bedroom key with her when she went to the hospital. I hadn't noticed it when I first used that keyring to open the front door, but there is a skeleton key. It does not, however, fit the bedroom door. Nor do any of the other skeleton keys I've thrown in the box of loose keys. *Shit, does this mean I'll never get into the room without taking the door down?*

Rather than fight with the actual door latch, I decide to try the padlock. As soon as I insert the first key, thunder shakes the house. *Is it supposed to rain today?* I hadn't thought to check the weather. Shrugging off the surprise, I try the next key. Another clap of thunder sounds loud enough to make me grit my teeth. The lack of windows in the hall keeps me from seeing outside or hearing any rain, but if the thunder is any indication, this storm will be a doozy. Hopefully, it'll be over before my friends get caught in it.

The second key fits into the lock, but it won't turn. Maybe the lock is just frozen shut after having been closed all these years. It isn't like Grandma Gretna just passed last week, or that she hadn't been sick for who knows how long beforehand. No one had given me any of those details, and I'm not sure I want to know. There's already been enough guilt about staying away from Colliers Town for so long.

"C'mon! It has to be one of these keys," I say to the empty house.

I try another in the lock, and it won't even slip into the keyhole. With a snarl, I slam my fist into the door repeatedly. The pounding, much like the thunder, echoes around me, as unyielding as my grandmother had been.

"Please let me in," I say, the whine in my voice an unlikely pairing with the previous moment of anger. "Even in death, you lock me out."

Tears fall as I pick up the second keyring and begin working through the keys. Who knows how much time passes before one finally slips into the lock with a satisfying click and turns smoothly, as if the lock itself had simply been waiting to open. I take a deep breath and try the doorknob. It still doesn't turn. The door, however, pushes open without so much as a creak, startling me to the point I nearly fall forward with it.

The room is unexpectedly cold considering the rest of the house stays at a comfortable 71 degrees. No light enters through the drapes. *They're probably the same ones as the dining room*, I muse. Whoever had created the material and sewn those things could've had a lucrative business in blackout curtains. Reaching around the door frame, I find a single light switch and flip it on.

Nothing happens.

I try again, not expecting anything different but needing to try anyway. Then I pull the drapes open, thinking to let in some light that way, but everything remains dark. Outside, a storm rages, and torrential rain pelts the windows. How thick are these windows that I've not heard the rain before? Again, I throw up a quick prayer that my friends are safe and will wait out the storm before trying to make it here for dinner. Hopefully, the storm ends before it gets too late.

Though I've gained no additional light from outside, other than the occasional flicker of lightning, my eyes adjust to the darkness enough for me to find lamps on either side of the four-post bed. Replacing the bulbs with extras I'd had Joanna bring earlier this week, I finally get my first real glimpse at the hidden parts of Grandma Gretna's life.

Besides the huge bed and its matching side tables, the master suite holds an antique secretary desk complete with the foldable cover that serves as both a writing surface and a security measure. No doubt the desk will be locked just as tightly as the room had been. *That's a tomorrow problem*, I think as I continue appraising the furniture. For example, the imposing dresser is at least as long as Jacob is tall and will need no fewer than four strong men to get it out of the room. That is, of course, assuming it will fit through the door. I can't help but wonder if my grandparents, or even my great grandparents, built the furniture inside the house. Every piece is massive.

As is true of all the bedrooms, there are no closets. Instead, there are two wardrobes on either side of the room, one set between the two windows. Thankfully, the storm is abating, and light has begun to trickle into the room from outside. Sweeping my eyes around one last time, I shake my head. All that anticipation. All the secrecy. I'm not sure what I'd expected to find once I got into the room, but the mundanity of it all leaves me weary.

When I enter the kitchen and grab my phone, I realize it's way past time to put the baked ziti in the oven. Jacob and Joanna are on the way. Good thing game night is already set up. Honestly, as much as I was yearning for an excuse to cook for the first time in weeks, I'm just happy for the company.

"We're so glad you're alright, Morgan," Jacob says as soon as he and Joanna enter the house. He walks toward me like he's going to grab me for a hug, but then he turns away. *Ouch*. I guess I deserve that after our last conversation, but still.

"There are trees down everywhere," Joanna adds, seemingly oblivious to the tension between Jacob and I.

"Including your driveway," he finishes without missing a beat.

My eyes bounce back and forth between them. I'd forgotten how seamlessly they finish each other's thoughts when they're excited or worried about something. It's nice to know they'd worried about me. No one has worried over me in a long time.

"Wait, you said there's a tree down on the way in here? How'd you get to the house, then?"

"Jacob has four-wheel drive. My car is sitting down near the street where we left it."

"I'll bring my chainsaw tomorrow when I come to do the porch. It'll be fine. We're just glad you're okay, and it seems like the house held up well."

"Honestly, I hardly even knew it was raining. If it hadn't been for some really loud claps of thunder, I might have missed the storm altogether." I laugh uncomfortably, and the twins both grimace at my poor attempt at humor.

I might never be a comedian, but I'm a damn good cook and can entertain in other ways. "How about a board game while we wait for the food to finish up?"

We settle on Life. I choose the path to college. Both Joanna and Jacob choose to start a career. Nothing like Life imitating, well, life. The rest of the night passes in a flurry of food, fun, and friendship. Laughter fills the once stuffy dining room, and genuine warmth settles in my chest for the first time in years. I'm home. I'm safe. I have people who care about me. Though I might not have believed it when I arrived a couple weeks ago, I'm glad to be back in Colliers Town, in this house.

CHAPTER FOURTEEN

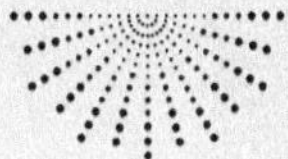

COURTING LONELINESS

*M*organ

I wake with a start. *What in the hell was that sound?* It happens again. A low whir that suddenly turns louder. *Is that a Chainsaw?*

"Jacob," I breathe out and scramble from bed to throw on some clothes.

Remembering the major storm we'd had yesterday, I grab my boots rather than my sneakers before heading down the stairs. He's here to help, but I don't want him to be doing all the work on the property alone. I don't want him to feel like I'm just using him, and I need to see the damage for myself. It's still unnerving that I couldn't hear the rain or see the lightning from the center of the house or my grandmother's room. I can only imagine what it looks like outside.

My eyes lock onto the dark wooden door at the end of the corridor while I put on my boots at the bottom of the stairs. There are secrets hidden in that ominous room; I just know it, but I can't go searching today. Today, Jacob is here to help clear the driveway and finish the back porch. I try to think about it as nothing more than a friendly gesture, but my heart flutters knowing he's out there already. My feet carry me toward the door, toward Jacob. As I reach for the knob, my phone dings.

JOANNA: Jake should be on his way there. I'll be by after church.

ME: Thanks, J. I hear the chainsaw now. See you soon.

JOANNA: ☺

The chainsaw starts back up as soon as I open the door. Though I can hear it clear as day, I can't see Jacob. The tree must have fallen further down the drive than I imagined. Cresting the hill that separates the house from the driveway, I catch a glimpse of tawny beige skin between the trees that line the curved gravel drive. I close the distance and stop. Jacob is shirtless, his jeans slung so low on his waist, I can see the dark trail of hair that leads from his belly button to his...*No, I will not think of that. I won't picture him naked in my bed.*

"Holy hell." My voice is breathy when he turns around, his tight ass on full display as he climbs up onto the tree trunk to remove another limb. As much as I try, I can't drag my eyes from him. He is all tight, sinewy muscle, and the muscles between my legs tighten watching him deftly make short work of the smaller branches along the downed tree's trunk.

It takes a moment for me to get myself together enough to call out, "Can I help?" while trying to make my voice project over the sound of the chainsaw. He doesn't immediately respond, so I step closer to the fallen tree and wave both my arms high. After a few seconds, he looks up and cuts off the chainsaw, a smile taking over his face.

"Good morning, beautiful. I hope I didn't wake you. I just wanted to make sure my sister could get up to the house when she comes by later."

I can't help but smile at him and his consideration. He'd always been such a great brother. He'd always been so good to me too. That was one of the reasons I'd kissed him that day when we were fourteen. He had once again protected me from bullies and made me feel valued. The kiss was a thank you of sorts, at least that's what I had told myself all those years ago, and over the years whenever I thought about Colliers Town.

"You did," I say with a wink before I think better of the innocent flirting, "but it's okay. I forgive you since you are out here playing Paul Bunyan in my driveway."

He laughs, and butterflies take flight in my stomach. He has a deep, rich laugh that sends shivers down my spine. I wonder at how much kinder the years have been to him than to me as I watch this fine specimen of a man stand atop the fallen tree like a god.

"Can I help?" I ask again, licking my lips to battle against how dry my mouth has gone.

A wicked grin takes over his face as he jumps down from the tree trunk. The tree is smaller around than I had originally thought considering the trouble it's causing for anyone wanting to get in or out of the driveway. The tree is all but forgotten when Jacob walks toward me, chainsaw hanging idly from his right hand, and I shudder at the gleam in his eye.

"Have you ever used a chainsaw, Morgan?"

I shake my head, gulping down the knot that forms as he draws closer. "No," I manage to squeak out. He walks around behind me, wrapping one arm around my waist and matching his other hand to mine. I gasp when he pulls me tightly against him, my breaths becoming erratic. He brings his mouth to the space where my neck and shoulder meet and inhales deeply. "Jacob?" My voice is barely a whisper, but I feel him smile against my skin in response.

"Grab the chainsaw right above my hand."

I look down to where his hands hold the apparatus and follow his directions. He tells me to grasp it tightly before he loosens his grip, allowing me to feel its full weight. It's much heavier than it looks, and I nearly drop it, but he's right there to wrap his hand back around the handle with mine.

"You will never need to hold or carry this thing with one hand, and when you use one, you will always use both hands. Want to give it a try?"

His lips are at my ear, yet I struggle to focus on his words. Heat pools in my core, and I wish he'd just drop that chainsaw and wrap his arms completely around me. He smiles again, his lips traveling down my neck.

"Jacob."

"I'm waiting for your answer, Morgan."

My answer? What had he asked? "What was the question?"

He chuckles against my skin. "Do you want to try cutting something with the chainsaw?"

"Oh, yes," I answer and quickly step away from him toward the tree, letting go of the chainsaw.

When I turn back toward him, he's standing in the same place watching me. I lift my hands in an outward gesture wondering why he hadn't followed.

"I thought we were going to cut something?"

He blinks a few times, as if coming out of a daze and then grins.

"Sorry, I got caught up watching you walk away. I've never seen leggings look so good."

"You're the worst," I say as a smile spreads across my face.

He starts the chainsaw as he walks toward me, and I shriek. I'm not at all afraid of Jacob, but the sound of the machine alongside the determined look in his eyes as he stalks toward me is unnerving.

"Come here," he says over the sound of the saw.

I follow his direction and stand in front of him. He once again instructs me to grab the chainsaw with one hand and reach around to place my other hand on the handle meant to steady it. My entire body vibrates, and not just from the hum of the saw. Jacob is once again pressed up against me, guiding me with his body to approach the tree. Now that I'm right next to it, I can easily tell that it's about three feet in diameter, a small tree compared to some of the others on the property.

Working together, we cut shallow slits into the wood, slowly widening them, so we can cut deeper. Once we make it halfway through the trunk, Jacob releases the saw to me, and I finish the job. In my excitement, I nearly drop the chainsaw, and he has to quickly grab it before it hits the ground.

"Give it here, muscles," he says, pride in his voice.

"That was awesome!"

Jacob barely has a chance to put the chainsaw down on the part of the trunk we've just separated from the rest when I throw my arms around his neck and jump into his embrace. The moment his hands grab my ass to hold me up, I realize what I've done, but it's too late. His lips are on mine, and my hands are in his hair, my legs wrapping around his waist.

"Morgan," he whispers against my mouth between breaths.

I rub my center against him as my hands run along his shoulders, my nails scratching trails along his skin. He kisses his way down my neck to my chest, and I've never been so grateful for the warmth of early fall that allowed me to come out in just a cami. Though I'm no longer young and perky, my tits are still full and mostly stay where they belong behind the fabric, even without a bra.

Without a word, he flips us around, so my ass is perched on the tree trunk. His hands, now free to roam, pull my top down, and his mouth captures one of my nipples while his fingers roll the other into a taut pebble. I moan and let my head flop backward, my hands holding his head to my breast. His mouth spins a web of heat around my body, and I arch against him, pressing my center into him, desperate to feel his hardness.

"Jacob," I purr, so deep in my arousal that I can't remember why I'd pushed him away the other morning.

"If we don't stop, I'm going to take you right here in plain view of the street."

Though his words are likely meant to tamp the desire near to overflowing, they have the opposite effect. Somehow, the idea of us getting caught as adults is like an aphrodisiac. We lost so much time together because of a simple kiss that I can't imagine a worse consequence, yet I'm easily able to picture an amazing release for us both.

"So?" I say, more as a challenge than a question.

His moan is almost a growl, as he reaches between us and rubs my mound through my pants. His thumbs slip into the waistband of my leggings, ready to pull them down, when the sound of tires on gravel hits our ears. I quickly release my legs, and he pulls my shirt back up in place. Magically, he pulls his t-shirt from somewhere and slides it over his head, covering the red marks my nails left in his back.

"Help me push this piece of trunk over to the tree line," he says, finally catching his breath.

I nod and turn toward the trunk, taking a deep breath before putting my hands on the bark. As the adrenaline wears off, my knees weaken. It's all I can do to stay standing, let alone actually put any effort into pushing the piece of trunk out of the way. Thankfully, Jacob is strong enough to do most of the work himself. He likely just asked for help to hide our activity from Joanna who's watching from her car, waiting for the opening, so she can pull up toward the house.

"Hey there, you two. It looks like you've been doing some work this morning." Joanna's voice is normal, yet I cringe as if each word is an accusation.

I force my voice to remain neutral. "Jake here did most of the work before I even came out of the house."

"Morgan got her first chance to run a chainsaw, with supervision, of course."

My nostrils flare at the obvious deepening of his drawl. With lips pursed, I turn on him.

"I might have figured it out on my own if I had to," I retort, and he holds his hands up in a placating gesture.

Joanna beeps her horn, and we both jump. "Can I get by now?"

We step out of the way and watch Joanna pull around the rest of the trunk still blocking the majority of the driveway. She drives to the top of the hill and drops out of sight toward the house. I make to follow her, but Jacob grabs my hand.

"Hey, are you okay? Are we okay?"

"Yeah," I respond quietly, not sure what else to say.

His eyes search mine. After a moment, he lets go with a nod and turns back toward the tree.

"I'm just going to cut off another chunk, so you have plenty of room to get around it in case you have to leave before I can get the rest. Then, I'll be up there to finish the porch."

I watch him pick up the chainsaw and wish we could go back to the moment right before Joanna arrived. Things are much simpler in the moments of passion when emotions are isolated to our groins rather than drowning in the sea of doubt that is our brains, or my brain, at least.

"You don't have to try and do everything in one day, you know," I say with as nonchalant a manner as possible. "You have to go to work tomorrow and don't need to be sore from helping me out."

He turns abruptly, his gaze firm. "I can handle it, Morgan."

My sharp inhale is audible to my own ears, and by the change in his expression, he heard it too. We stare at each other for what feels like forever before I turn to jog back toward the house.

CHAPTER FIFTEEN

CLEARING THE AIR

Jacob

Morgan drops out of sight, and I growl in frustration. Without a thought, I turn around and kick the tree at my feet, stomping my sole into the trunk's side. It doesn't even budge, and I can't help but think how fitting that response is. I know she isn't ready in the same way I am. Hell, she told me so directly. Still, I couldn't help myself when she jumped into my arms, pressing herself against me. "Great job, Asshole," I tell myself before restarting the chainsaw and clearing the path enough for her to get through over the next few days.

When I get to the house, Morgan and Joanna have already begun painting the entry. It's amazing how much brighter the space looks with a lighter color paint. "Looking good, ladies." Of course, I mean the work they're doing, but I throw a wink Morgan's way just to see her blush. The slight hint of pink reminds me of when we were kids. Even before there was anything between us, all it would take was a look and a wink to make her blush. It feels good to know that hasn't changed between us. I can be patient with the rest. Hell, I've waited twenty years already.

The back porch is nearly finished when Joanna and Morgan

enter the kitchen. I peek around the door frame from where I've been laying the new flooring to see Morgan bent over inside the fridge. Her ass in those leggings is going to be the death of me. When I lean up to adjust my hardening dick, everything in my tool belt shifts, and she whirls around to catch me watching. I smile until Joanna steps between us.

"Looking good in here, little brother."

The last part is a rib. Even at our grown-up age of 35, she loves to throw out the fact that she's slightly older than I am. We're fucking twins. It's not necessary. She's older, and I'm taller. What difference does it make?

"Stop scowling," she says. Though her voice is even, there's a smirk on her lips, and I draw my brows down more. "You're getting too old to be scowling like that. Those frown lines will be scaring off the children soon." Then she cackles and steps out of view.

I take a deep breath and let it out slowly. Sisters can be a real pain in the ass sometimes. Looking down at the floor, I wonder whether Morgan would notice if I pull up a few of the boards and bury Joanna under them. Of course, I won't do that, but a guy can fantasize, can't he?

"It does look good," Morgan says from behind me. "Thank you so much for all the work you've put into this. Guests are going to love coming out here to look out at the mountains. And it was a great idea to expand it, so we can have different types of seating like in the dining room."

Though she hasn't said anything that's untrue or irrelevant, I can tell she's rambling. Our moment from earlier has her rattled, and I'd be lying if I said knowing she's also affected doesn't make me happy. The woman does things to my heart and my body that are so far out of my control, I think I may be losing my mind. The thing is I don't want to stay sane if that's the case.

She takes a giggling breath like she's finally realized she's been talking a mile a minute before saying much more calmly, "Are you hungry? I was about to heat up the leftover ziti."

My smile is wide when I nod my head yes. "Let me finish this row of planks and clean myself up," I say before she retreats. My stomach growls, reminding me that I haven't eaten yet today, but I'd have dropped everything at her invitation anyway. I would drop everything if only she'd ask me.

Stepping into the kitchen, I see that they have set up a folding table in the middle of the room. It looks as out of place as her grandmother's spindle-legged table had seemed the first time I entered the house. She needs something more substantial, something worthy of the delicious meals she'll prepare here. I know she's planning to change out the cabinets, expand the pantry, and put in a bigger stove, but she's not said anything about a table.

"What do you plan to put here?" I ask, gesturing toward the eyesore in the middle of the floor, my nose wriggling.

Morgan looks between me and the table while Joanna chuckles off to the side. "I haven't decided yet," she says. Then she sighs. "Truthfully, I just haven't seen anything that fits what I want this space to do."

"Maybe you just need to have something custom made," I offer with a wink, hoping she gets the message.

"What do you suggest?"

Anything that will keep you inviting me to this house for however long it takes for you to realize I'd do anything for you. I don't say the words aloud, but I stare deeply into her eyes when I say, "Let me surprise you."

*M*organ
The house feels even emptier after Joanna and

Jacob leave, no matter how awkward their visit might've been. Today's awkwardness came in the way Jacob looked at me with heat in his eyes every couple of minutes. Admittedly, our time against the tree was hotter than hot, and I certainly wouldn't have stopped whatever had been about to happen had Joanna not showed up. But once she arrived, I tried to forget the moment happened, or at least I tried to put it in the back of my mind. His looks, though, made it nearly impossible.

Even when Joanna admitted to occasional loneliness and how grateful she is that we get to hang out regularly, Jacob's eyes pinned me with longing. What happened to taking our time to learn each other again? Part of me wishes I could be just as secure about us as he is, but the rest of me holds tight to reality. We're virtually strangers. Though I've told him about my estrangement from my husband, I'm not sure he realizes I'm still technically married. No papers have been signed.

A ding breaks through my thoughts, turning my attention from the ceiling that needs a fresh coat of paint. I try to ignore it, opting for companionable silence with the house. Then it dings two more times. Text messages. I grab the phone from the bedside table and glance at the unknown number.

> UNKNOWN NUMBER: It's Jake. Joanna gave me your number in case something happens at the house, and you need help.

> UNKNOWN NUMBER: I know it's getting late, but I wanted to make sure you had my number.

> UNKNOWN NUMBER: I hope you don't regret this morning, Morgana. I can't stop thinking about it.

I lay the phone on my chest, willing my heart to stop racing. Another ding forces my hand. I can't bring myself to completely ignore him. I never could years ago, and I can't do so now. I open the phone and save his number into my contacts before reading his last message.

JACOB: I know you asked for a restart. It's just
so hard when I've spent all these years thinking
about you.

ME: I understand that. I really do.

JACOB: You just don't feel the same.

ME: It's not about how I feel, Jacob. It's about
what I know to be true.

JACOB: I'm obviously attracted to you. Still.
Time hasn't changed that.

ME: Attraction isn't enough. My impending
divorce is proof of that fact. I can't deal with
any more loss.

JACOB: There's nothing you can do to lose me
again. I'm not a kid anymore, and this time, I
will follow you anywhere.

Tears sting my eyes, and I struggle to see the screen clearly. My breath hitches. How is he still the same Jacob, and I'm nowhere near the same Morgan? When I don't respond right away, he apologizes for pushing too hard. I still have no words, and the tears flow more freely.

JACOB: Hey, let's table this, ok. We can talk
about something else. Did you know the Fall
Festival opens next weekend?

I wipe at my eyes, trying to clear my vision enough to make sure I've read the message correctly. The Fall Festival? I'd never been able to attend any festival or even the fair with my friends as a kid. Truth be told, even as an adult, I've only been once or twice because my husband wanted to go. He never wanted to do any of the fun stuff, though, only eat.

ME: You and J still go each year?

JACOB: Of course! Want to go?

ME: Yes!!

JACOB: :)

ME: Now get some sleep. You have work in the morning.

JACOB: Ok Morgana. Good night.

ME: Night

CHAPTER SIXTEEN

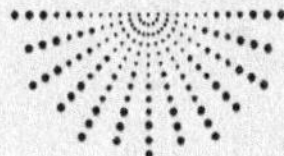

THE FALL FESTIVAL

*M*organ

The week passes in a blur, all of my energy focused on the excitement of going to the festival with my best friends. I can't remember the last time I'd anticipated something more. I even talk myself out of going back into my grandmother's suite this week because I don't want anything to spoil the mood.

Every evening when Joanna stops by, we talk about the things we hope to do or see there. Joanna's most excited about the bands that will be playing. According to what she's seen in the newspaper, a band out of Florida is headlining opening night, which is when we've all agreed to go.

"What's Jake's favorite part of the Fall Festival?" I ask.

Every time I ask a question about Jacob, I try to keep my voice neutral, and then guilt kicks in. I don't like hiding things from Joanna, especially not about my feelings for Jacob. Lately, though, Joanna has started giving me a sideways glance every time I do it.

"You do know that I've always known you and Jake had a thing for each other? At least, I've always been privy to his feelings for you."

My eyes go wide, and I stammer. "I...I'm...I don't know what you're talking about."

Joanna rolls her eyes. "You're not going to hurt my feelings or our friendship because you like my brother. At least, not unless you intentionally hurt him. I see the way you two look at each other, and I don't see that happening. I'm kinda jealous."

"There's nothing between Jake and I. We're just friends, like you and I are friends. You two are my best friends."

"Whatever, Morgan. Anyway, he loves the haunted hayride and that one ride that spins you so fast you can pull your feet off the ground and turn upside down without falling."

I nearly choke on the soda I had just taken a sip of. "There's a ride you stand up on and float in the air?"

"No, silly. You stick to the wall. Have you never ridden the rides?"

A deep sigh leaves my lips. "As you know, my grandmother never let me go, and mom couldn't afford it. My husband only wanted to go and eat, so I learned to pretend the rides weren't there."

"Oh, hell no. You're better off without that stick in the mud. I mean, the food is ok, but the shows and the rides are where it's at!"

Every evening, Joanna tells me about the different attractions at the festival, and I make a mental note of the ones I want to try. Guilt claws at me that they have to treat me to the event, but Jacob makes it clear each night when we fall asleep texting that he's calling this a date.

By the time Saturday afternoon comes, I'm absolutely giddy. I keep having to wipe my hands on my shorts and reapply my lipstick because I've chewed it off. Not only am I going to have fun with my friends, but I'll be on a date with Jacob and get to try so many new things. Jacob picks me up on the way to get Joanna, and we make the hour-long drive singing along to the radio and talking about the different concerts Jacob and Joanna have seen there over the years.

"We may be a small county in the middle of nowhere," Jacob says, "but we've had some amazing bands come through for the festival each year."

"I feel like I've missed out on so much over the years."

Jacob reaches over and entwines his fingers with mine. "We have plenty of time left to make more memories, better memories."

"Yeah," Joanna says, co-signing his sentiment. "Besides, many of those years would have been a wash anyway. Neither your grandmother nor your mom would have taken you or let you go with us. So better that we all go now as adult friends. We can just act like children."

We all laugh and then enjoy the companionable silence that falls between us for the remainder of the trip. As soon as Jacob parks, we make a beeline for the food stations. There are vendors lined up around the perimeter of the festival, and we peruse every option.

"Funnel cake," I yell, pulling on their arms. "I haven't had funnel cake in so long."

We walk up to the vendor and greet the older woman taking orders from across the tables that serve as a barrier. We order three chicken sandwiches and a funnel cake.

"Wyatt, I need three grilled with cheese. I also need one funnel cake with just powdered sugar, Rayna." The two people toward the back of the tent acknowledge the orders and begin moving around. "Are you sure you don't want any chocolate syrup or whipped cream on that cake?"

"No, thank you," Jacob and I say at the same time.

The old woman smiles at us. "Where did y'all come in from?"

"Colliers Town, on the other side of the lake," Joanna responds, looking past the woman at the ass of the guy working the grill.

When the younger woman, Rayna, turns around to pass us the funnel cake, Joanna takes a step back. I catch the woman's barely whispered, "he's not on the menu," and nearly burst out laughing.

"I'll take that plate of yumminess, thanks." I grab the funnel cake, immediately pulling off a piece of the sweet confection and popping it into my mouth.

"Hey, give me a piece of that," Joanna says, following me over to a table that had just emptied.

"That chick wanted to gouge out your eyeballs, J. Must be her man you were ogling."

"I wasn't ogling, exactly, but he does have a nice ass."

I shake my head and pass a piece of funnel cake to Jacob when he sits down with our sandwiches.

"You two are going to ruin your lunch eating all that sugar."

"Thanks, dad," Joanna says with an eye roll.

We all laugh and dig into the food. I feel Jacob's eyes on me every few seconds and try to focus on my meal while warmth creeps into my center.

"What should we do first?" I ask.

"I'm pretty sure the first performance doesn't start until 6pm, so we have some time for rides if that's what you want to do," Joanna offers.

"Yes," Jacob says, grabbing my hand and pulling me toward the tilt-a-whirl as soon as we throw our trash in the bin.

We ride the rides for the next hour straight. Finally, after the third time on the Graviton, Joanna taps out. She opts for a seat on a bench near the main stage arguing that she'll hold seats for us until the concerts start.

"Are you sure? We can sit with you until you're ready to go again," Jacob says, his hand on my waist as we both look at Joanna with worried expressions.

"I'm fine, just tired of spinning in circles. Go, enjoy! Maybe when dusk comes, we can do the haunted hayride."

"Oh fun!" I exclaim, clapping my hands together.

"Okay," Jacob says, "we'll be back in less than an hour to watch the concert with you."

Joanna smiles and shoos us away with a wave of her hands. We run hand-in-hand to the other side of the festival to try some of the rides there. With the lines, there won't be much time to enjoy ourselves before the concerts start if we don't rush.

When we get back, Joanna is chatting with some strange dude neither of us recognize, which is clearly obvious from Jacob's scowl. Joanna's eyes are bright, and she throws her head back in laughter at something the guy says. I can't help but smile at my friend's obvious flirtation, but when Joanna runs her hand down the guy's arm, I have to run to catch up to Jacob before he interrupts them.

Joanna's eyes widen, taking in her brother's expression and stance. "Oh, hey, Jake. Morgan. This is Archer. He's here at the lake with some friends."

Archer reaches out a hand to Jacob who doesn't acknowledge him at all, all of his attention focused on Joanna. I reach between the two men and take the offered hand.

"Hi there. I'm the awkward best friend."

My voice pulls Jacob from his trance, and his attention turns to me and then to where my hand is settled in Archer's. I pull away, hoping I haven't made the moment worse. Finally, Jacob looks at the man.

"My sister says you're here on vacation with some friends?" His eyebrow raises, and I can read the challenge in it.

"Yeah. My buddy Gage just got divorced, and we're here to celebrate."

Jacob looks around. "You look pretty alone here for a celebratory group."

Archer stands. "Joanna, thanks for helping me pass the time. I really enjoyed you," he says, taking Joanna's hand.

Jacob's body tenses, and I touch his arm.

"Hey there, why don't we go take that hayride now that the sun is setting?"

I lean in close trying to take his attention away from Joanna and Archer. When Jacob's eyes finally find mine, I smile and grab his hand, pulling him toward the forest where the hayride starts. Before we get too far away, I look back at Joanna and wink. My friend laughs, mouthing a quick thank you before turning back to Archer.

"Don't think I don't know that you pulled this stunt to distract me from my sister and that vagabond," Jacob says, but there's no heat in his words.

I laugh. "Vagabond? Seriously, Jacob? Who says that anymore?"

I wrap my arm around his and look up into his eyes while we walk.

CHAPTER SEVENTEEN

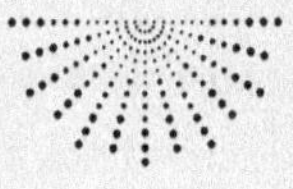

AN INFERNO

$\mathcal{M}$organ

The line for the haunted hayride is surprisingly short, and we only have to wait one full turn before climbing onto the trailer pulled behind the huge tractor. There's no hay on the trailer, just wooden seats built into the sides with plenty of walking space in the middle. Within the first five minutes of the ride, I learn why they've left so much unused space when three men with modified chainsaws come running from behind the tall trees and jump onto the trailer with us. They taunt us with the loud machines, touching the floor with them, so the entire trailer shakes. I'm not exactly scared, but I'm also not a fan of having a chainsaw pressed to the floor between my legs. It's unnerving, and when I let out a small squeak, Jacob pulls me tight against him with a low chuckle.

As the ride continues and adrenaline pumps through my veins, I press myself even further against Jacob. Each time a scream or bang happens in the dark, I jump, and he presses a kiss to the top of my head. By the time we make it through half of the circuit, my entire body has turned toward him, and he's pulled my legs across his lap. The ride is well-choreographed because I never get the opportunity to catch my breath or calm my heart rate. Being pressed up against Jacob doesn't help either of those situations either. The warm night feels even warmer wrapped in his arms, and I consider climbing into his lap completely multiple times.

Suddenly, the woods go quiet. No actors jump out at us. No animatronics blow smoke. No one calls out for help within the woods. Then, the tractor stops and the old driver yells. "What the hell?" As the other riders stand to look around the huge wheels, Jacob holds me to him and leans back to look from the side of the trailer.

"There's a fire," he whispers against my ear.

"A fire?" I ask aloud, willing him to repeat the words to ensure I've heard him correctly.

"A fire?" Others on the ride repeat, some jumping off the back to run toward the main fairgrounds.

"Joanna!" I cry out, concern taking over.

"Shhh," Jacob soothes. "From what I can see, the fire is near the food tents, not the concert stage. My sister would not leave the music once it's started."

"Are you sure? Should we go try to help?"

"Morgan, everyone ran that direction. We'll just be in the way." He holds my face between his hands.

I look into his eyes, and his calmness in the midst of the chaos, has me nodding in agreement. He's probably right.

"Now, how about we talk about your little squeaks and screams at each jump scare," he teases, nuzzling his nose where my neck and shoulder meet.

"Jacob, what are you doing?"

"Taking advantage of everyone else's distraction. Let me distract you."

*J*acob

I take Morgan's chin in my hand and turn her face so that I can press my lips to hers. When she doesn't pull away, I take it as a sign to push further. Rubbing my tongue against the seam of her lips, I coax her to open for me, and she does with a sigh. My hands rub up and down her back. When she's settled into our kiss, I pull her around until she's straddling my legs, her heat pressing into me. God, I wish she had worn a dress instead of these tight jean shorts. Though I've loved the way they fit her ass just right, they don't allow the convenience of access I really want. They're too tight to slip to the side, and her shirt is too short to slip them off completely.

"Want to play a game in the dark?"

"A game?" she asks. Her eyes are like coals in the darkness where the only parts shining are from the moon reflecting in their depths.

I nod against her neck where I trail kisses up to her ear, nipping at the sensitive skin right below her lobe. The things I want to do to her are not meant for public consumption, but we are alone on this hayride. Everyone else is off gawking at or helping with the fire, yet the only fire I'm worried about is the one radiating from between Morgan's legs.

"Do you feel how hard you make me, Morgana?"

She rubs herself against me, pushing her hips back and forth until I moan and grab her. She's crazy if she thinks she can give me the night I'd been dreaming about for two decades and then force me to stay away only to dry hump me now. Oh no, she's going to get everything I've been holding onto while waiting for her all this time. I just have to make sure it's in a way that makes her happy. She comes first and will always come first.

"Jacob," she says on a whisper, her undulations seeming to have an equally erotic effect on her too.

"What do you need from me?"

"I want you to touch me, please."

I smile against her ear at those sweet, sweet words. "How? With what? Tell me what you want, and I will give it to you."

"I want you to use your hands."

"And do what with them?" I run my hands through her hair, grasping it near her scalp, pulling only slightly until her mouth opens in surprise. My tongue tangles with hers, and I nip at her lip until she's panting in my grasp. "Was that it?"

"No. I mean yes. No, I mean no. I want your fingers on my pussy. Rub my clit."

"Ah, there are the words I've been wanting to hear. Turn around."

I release her hair and help her to stand. Before she can turn, I unbutton her shorts, the five open buttons loosening them enough they nearly slide off her hips on their own. I want her completely naked, but I won't take the chance someone comes back to the trailer and sees her that way. I'd have to kill them, and I've been without her for too many years to go to jail and once again be without her.

I turn her around and sit her on my lap between my open legs, so her back is against my chest. My hands massage her breasts through her shirt while I kiss along the back and sides of her neck, pulling her earlobe into my mouth. Her soft moans have me rock hard and ready to be inside of her.

"Jacob, please," she whines, and I chuckle.

"Okay, impatient one, let me give you what you need."

I slide one hand down her abdomen, grazing my fingers against her shirt, pressing firmly enough for her to feel the trail. When my hand slides inside of her shorts, I find that her clit is already swollen with need, and her panties are soaked.

"Fuck, you're already so damn wet. I want to taste you!"

She sucks in a breath. "How? Out here?"

I chuckle again. "If I were sure no one would come back, I'd have you naked and spread out before me like a fucking buffet. Do you have any idea how long I waited and dreamed of your sweet taste? Now that I've had it, I crave it." She squirms, rubbing her thighs together, trying to build friction with my fingers, but I haven't fully sunk them between her lips yet. "Give me your hand," I say.

She puts her hand in mine, and I slide it down into her shorts, replacing my fingers with hers. Her breath hitches, and I kiss her neck, running my tongue from her earlobe to the spot where her neck meets her shoulder before sucking the sensitive skin there. I push her fingers between her sweet lips and onto her clit. She moans, and I close my eyes at both the sound of her pleasure and the feel of her arousal. Her hips rotate up to meet our hands, and her grinding on my lap is making me crazy. I'm going to have her right here.

"Jacob. I need your fingers in me."

"Rub your clit for me, baby. Fuck my fingers and make yourself come."

I push my fingers inside of her, and she sighs in pleasure. She feels so good, and I can hardly wait to replace my fingers with my dick. She does as I say and rubs her clit in soft circles while small mewling noises come from her lips.

"That's it, Morgana. Work those magic fingers."

My fingers plunge in and out of her in long, slow strokes before I curl them up to find the spot that will send her over the edge. I push further inside of her and rub her inner ridge while she rubs the outer.

"Let me taste your fingers," I say, and she freezes for a second. "Don't freeze up on me now, Morgana. I need you to come all over me, soaking my hand. But I also need to taste your sweetness."

She slowly withdraws her fingers from where they've been working her clit into a frenzy, matching my internal strokes. She turns her head slightly, trying to look into my eyes, and I lick along her jawline before kissing it.

"Look at how wet those fingers are," I whisper against her cheek.

Morgan's hips rock back and forth, rubbing my cock through my jeans. I won't last long. When she puts her fingers in my mouth, I close my lips around them, sucking in the delicious nectar. At the same time, I pump in and out of her pussy harder, and her moans become louder. With my free hand, I turn her face and put her fingers into her own mouth.

"Lick them clean for me. You taste so fucking good, don't you?"

She nods, and I growl at how unexpectedly and deliciously naughty my Morgana is. All the years I'd been hoping to find her again, wanting to make her mine, I still pictured her as that repressed little girl I'd known. The woman she's become while away is even better. She's everything I could have imagined, and everything about her makes me ache to make her mine. I just need her to agree.

Within seconds, she throws her head back, and I clamp my hand over her mouth to silence her screams. I don't want anyone running this way thinking they needed to save her when I'm giving her exactly what she's asked for.

"That's it, Morgana. Fuck, you're so goddamn sexy! Are you read for me, baby?"

"Huh?" she asks, her head still laid back against my shoulder while her breaths become more controlled.

"Lift up a second, Morgana. We're going to do a magic trick."

I smile against her neck when she absently follows my directions. I slip her shorts down and my dick out.

"Jacob, what are you doing?" Her head turns from side to side like she's looking for people to come out of the woods.

"It's not what I'm doing, sweetheart. It's what you're going to do."

With one hand, I grab my shaft, holding it in place, while the other reaches around her, sliding my hand between her legs to guide her onto me. A small moan escapes her lips as soon as I find her entrance. She doesn't try to pull away or stop the momentum. Instead, she slides herself fully onto me until her bare ass lands on my groin, the length of my dick buried completely within her. I let out a groan of satisfaction at finally having her squeezing around me. I've jerked off so often to the memory of our one night together weeks ago, but no memories, dreams, or self-soothing could take the place of this right here. And when she started moving her hips, my eyes roll back into my head.

*M*organ

The fullness of him inside of me is overwhelming. I'd been blinded by lust and memories and decades-old longing to fully stay in the moment the last time. Now, here, in this moment, Jacob is everything. The initial fear of being caught dissipates the second his cock stretches my entrance. My body craves him, every nerve-ending firing, sending shockwaves of need straight to my pussy. I don't even care about whether or not I'm fully prepared for him, don't care about any potential discomfort. I just need to feel him inside of me, and now that he's here, I want more. My hips rock of their own accord, and my walls clench, holding him tightly. Using the seat for leverage, I lift myself off of his shaft until just the tip remains before seating him back inside fully. My thighs will be screaming in the morning, but for now, it's my core that needs attention.

Behind me, Jacob moans softly with every move. Though he holds onto my hips, he doesn't try to take over, instead letting me set the pace. I lean back against his chest and make circles with my hips until Jacob moans my name.

"Fuck, Morgana. That's so fucking good!"

His sounds of pleasure coupled with the feel of his cock inside my pussy and the painfully tight grip on my hips sends shockwaves through my body, moving me closer to the explosion I need. I bounce up and down on his cock with short strokes until Jacob's breaths come out like panting.

"Yes, baby, ride my dick. Take what you need."

I moan at the building pressure and his praise. My strokes slow until I find the rhythm and angle that has his tip rubbing my spot. Within moments, I'm so close to finishing, I'm whimpering with the need to release.

"That's it, my little witch, I feel you tightening around me. Are you ready?"

"Yes, fuck. I need to come."

Jacob leans back, lifting his pelvis until my feet no longer touch the boards on the bottom of the trailer, and he begins rocking his hips to pump in and out of me at a grueling pace. My moans break off when he reaches between my legs and begins rubbing my clit as he plows in and out of me.

"Jacob," I cry.

"That's it, baby, come for me. Squeeze my dick and take me with you!"

I do as he commands, my walls pulsing, the spasms wracking my body until I think I'll lose consciousness. He buries his face in my hair and cries out his own release. I feel him pumping into me, and the realization that we haven't used any protection swims through my mind alongside the acknowledgment that I don't care. I belong to Jacob. I've always belonged with him. The past 20 years had just been a delay of the inevitable.

Once we're dressed again, we head toward the restrooms hand in hand before finding Joanna who is dancing in the arms of that guy we'd left her with nearly two hours ago.

"You ready to go?" I ask her. When she jumps out of the guy's arms, I giggle. Jacob just scowls at the other man from my side.

"What the hell, Morgan? And where have you two been?" She

asks the question as if she'd actually been looking for us. I eye her skeptically, and she looks away.

"On the hayride," Jacob says with a shrug.

Joanna turns her gaze to him, disbelief written in the look. "That ride stopped a long time ago when that stupid dog started a fire in the chicken and funnel cake tent."

"Oh, is that where the fire was?" I ask, heat rushing into my cheeks as my voice squeaks with too much enthusiasm.

Joanna narrows her eyes, and I look toward the guy standing behind her. "How have the bands been?"

He just smiles and shrugs, his gaze going back to Jacob. Jacob continues sending daggers his way, obviously making the guy uncomfortable.

"You've got my number, beautiful. Use it," he says and kisses her cheek before walking off.

We wait while Joanna watches him walk away. He joins a group of guys standing up near the stage where a band called Blue Nitro is playing. At least, I assume that's their name thanks to the sign and logo painted on the bass drum. The crowd seems to really be feeling them, and I almost feel guilty at pulling my friend away. I'll ask for details about Joanna's new 'friend' when Jacob isn't around.

"Let's go," Jacob says, his voice much harder than it should be. He just came for fuck's sake.

"Relax, baby. Your little sister is just as full grown as we are." I draw out 'little' to emphasize the irony of his behavior. They're fucking twins, and he's the younger of the two by six minutes.

He grunts a non-response and walks toward the parking lot. I put my arm around Joanna's shoulders and give her a conspiratorial smile.

"I can't wait to hear all about him," I say.

"I can't wait to hear about this hayride...even if it was with my brother." Joanna rolls her eyes dramatically, and we both laugh the rest of the way to the truck.

CHAPTER EIGHTEEN

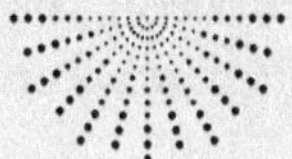

BREAKING BARRIERS

*J*acob

I wake to the sound of Morgan's vibrating phone. She's wrapped tightly in my arms, and when she doesn't stir, I'm afraid to reach for the unwanted tormentor for fear of waking her. When the vibrations stop, I let out a sigh of relief. It doesn't last long, though, because my phone starts ringing loudly from behind me on the nightstand. I reach my arm back behind me, nearly toppling the device to the floor before I grab it and pull it to my ear. How in the hell I manage to answer without even looking, I'll never know.

"What?...Joanna, slow down...what do you mean?...Are you sure?...I'll tell her."

I close my eyes with an audible groan before tossing the phone behind me and pulling Morgan close again. She turns her head to look at my face, and worry is written in her beautiful eyes.

"What was that all about? Is everything okay with your dad? Joanna?"

I stop her with a kiss before she can ramble on. She responds immediately, pressing her body against mine. Her nipples harden as soon as my hand slides up her torso, and she wraps her arms around my neck, deepening the kiss. My erection presses into her thigh where I've wrapped my legs around hers. I dip my head, pulling her nipple into my mouth and grazing it with my teeth, and she moans. That moan sends desire coursing straight to my cock. I have no doubt that if I reach between her legs, I'll find her wet and ready. Trailing kisses up her neck, I quickly cover her mouth with mine again, entwining my tongue with hers. Just as suddenly, I release a frustrated growl and lean my forehead against her temple.

"What's wrong?"

"I had every intention of waking up this morning and making love to you for hours. Joanna just said that won't be possible."

Morgan's brows draw together, confusion spreading across her face. The crease deepens the longer it takes for me to elaborate. I don't really want to even say the words, but there's no way to avoid it. I give her a wry smile of apology.

"Joanna said she tried to call you first, but you didn't answer."

Morgan nods at the unspoken question. "I thought you were still sleeping and didn't want to wake you trying to stretch for my vibrating phone."

I snort out a derisive laugh. "I shouldn't have answered mine."

"Please tell me what's going on. Why do you sound so dejected? You were setting me on fire just a few moments ago, even after talking to your sister, and now it's like you've been hosed down."

"Sorry. I. Fuck. Joanna said there was some guy in the store this morning asking about you and where he could find you."

Her brows come together again. "Some guy? You're acting like this over some random guy? You know everyone I know here and then some."

"No, not some random guy," I say, rising from the bed and slipping into my jeans from last night.

I put my hands on the top of her dresser and take in a deep breath before turning back to her. She's now sitting up in the bed, obviously uncomfortable with my silence. I know she can tell something's wrong, but I have no idea how to form the words.

"Talk to me, Jacob."

"Your..." I swallow as bile burns my throat. "Your husband is here in town. Joanna said she told him your address, and he's on his way here."

"My husband? Richard is on his way here? What the hell? Why?"

She gives me a questioning glance, and I shrug. I have no idea why he's on his way here. I don't know the man.

"Wait," she says, "are you worried about Richard?" She climbs out of the bed, and without covering herself, walks around to where I'm standing and grabs my hands. "Jacob, he's an egotistical jerk, and I want nothing to do with him."

"He obviously came all this way for a reason, Morgan."

She puts her arms around my torso, pulling me tight against her. Her body must think the skin-to-skin connection means something else because her nipples harden, making it hard for me to focus on anything besides the heat coming from between her legs. This woman is everything I've ever wanted, and I meant what I said last night. I will do whatever it takes to keep her this time. There's no telling why that man has driven himself all the way out here, but it will take an act of God for me to let her go. Still, I can't pretend that this impromptu visit hasn't thrown me for a loop.

Morgan kisses my chest where her head rests. Then she trails more kisses along my collar bone, and I let out a shaky breath. She reaches up and places her hands on either side of my face, drawing my gaze down to hers. "I don't care why he's here, Jacob. I'm not interested. I was done with him long before I knew you were still here. Long before I felt your lips on mine. Long before I'd gotten a taste of how perfectly we fit together. I was done with him long before I realized my heart has always been yours."

My eyes widen at her confession, and she gives me a sheepish smile. I lean down and brush my lips against hers. Then, I fist both hands in her hair and crush my mouth onto hers, silently commanding her to open. She does, and I revel in her words, in her acceptance of us, and in the love I feel in her kiss.

A sound from the driveway breaks through the haze of emotions swirling between us. A car approaches the house at a speed much quicker than necessary.

"Get dressed," I say, grabbing my t-shirt and boots from the floor. "I'll answer the door."

I'm out of the room and down the stairs before she can respond. My mind plays over all the possible ways I can answer the door. Part of me wants to attack him for showing up uninvited when he's the one who let her go. His idiocy deserves a busted jaw. Another part of me wants to gloat in triumph because she is mine. When he finally knocks on the door, I do neither of those things. I simply smile and say, "Morgan will be downstairs in a minute. She's getting dressed," enjoying the way his jaw tics.

CHAPTER NINETEEN

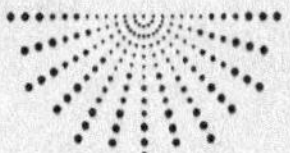

FUCK YOUR APOLOGY

*M*organ

I don't think I've ever gotten dressed so quickly before. All I can think of is Jacob beating the shit out of the kids who made fun of me. I don't think Richard would be that dumb, but he had said some pretty hurtful things to me before he asked for the divorce. There's no doubt in my mind, Jacob would swing first and ask questions later. Years ago, that behavior earned him a warning to control his temper. Today, it'll get him arrested on assault charges, and I can't take that chance. I'm running down the stairs barefoot, flip-flops in hand, just in time for Jacob to tell Richard I'm getting dressed. I can hear the taunt in his tone, and my stomach sinks.

I drop the shoes, slip my feet into them, and round the corner to find the men in a staring contest. Jacob leans against the setting room door frame, trying to appear nonchalant, but I feel the tension radiating from him. Richard stands just inside the door, eyes narrowed, and head tilted. He has a large envelope held at his side. His other hand, his dominant hand, is loosely sheathed in his pants pocket. It's been nearly a year since I've seen him, but he has changed. He's still attractive, in that older man who takes care of himself way, and his pants are perfectly tailored. He'd never worn tailored pants before. That must be his new girlfriend's doing. There's more gray in his hair, but it adds to the sophisticated look he's attempting to pull off by slicking it back. When he looks up, registering me standing in the hallway, the smugness oozing from him serves as a reminder of the man he is versus the man he presents to others.

"Richard," I say with a cheeriness I don't feel. "What brings you to Colliers Town?" As if possible, his eyes narrow even more. "If you were thinking about a fall vacation to the country, I'm sorry, but I don't have the house ready for customers yet."

Richard takes a step toward me, and Jacob steps away from the doorframe, standing at his full height. He's at least three inches taller than Richard's 5' 11" frame. Has Jacob always been that tall? It's hard to judge from my barely 5' 5" on a good day height. What isn't hard to judge, and obviously not hard for Richard either, is the menace in Jacob's stance.

"Can you call off your guard dog?" Richard asks with a sneer. "If you don't mind," he says directly to Jacob, "I'd like to have a conversation with my wife."

Jacob takes a deep breath. I watch his chest rise and fall before I step forward to intervene.

"You must have made a wonderfully pleasant impression on Joanna at the hardware store. She told Jacob you were on your way here."

Richard looks back at Jacob, his head cocking to the side slightly. Recognition of them as siblings must register because his eyes go wide. Without giving him a chance to say anything, I once again ask why he's here.

"Like I said, I wanted to talk to you. In private, if I could."

I shake my head, "You can't. You had plenty of time for that before."

"Morgan," he croons, his voice supplicating, but I know it's a ruse.

"Say what you have to say, Richard, and let me get on with my day."

"Can we at least sit down while we talk?"

I roll my eyes before moving to the side of the hall and gesturing toward the kitchen. Richard walks past me, casting his eyes down on me for a split second, so quick I almost question whether it had happened. He takes a seat at the head of the wooden island I'd commissioned Jacob to build for the space. My grandmother's large kitchen table was just too big for the room and not as functional as the island with its countertop height and lip on three sides to accommodate barstools for the staff I'm hoping to hire. I'd much rather have family-style meals and meetings around this island than around the foreboding table in the formal dining room. Actually, I've contemplated removing that table completely and setting up smaller eating spaces within the large room, so families and couples could remain in their intimate groups should they choose. Maybe I'll include one larger table, or a high-top counter for those who might want to sit and eat with others. I haven't yet told Jacob or Joanna my plan for the house. Truthfully, I'm a little worried they'll think I'm crazy for wanting to bring something like that into Colliers Town where nothing ever happens.

"Morgan," Richard starts, interrupting my reverie. He looks up at Jacob who is, once again, leaning against the door frame rather than taking a seat. Richard makes a disgruntled sound in the back of his throat but returns his attention to me. "Look, I know things went south there at the end. I could have handled your emotions better."

"My emotions? You could have handled my emotions better?" Though my tone is incredulous, he looks surprised at my response. "Your absolute inability to feel empathy is what made things extra difficult at the end. I lost my mother and my grandmother within the same year. Then while I was suffering, yes suffering, through a bout of depression, I found out that my husband of ten years was having an affair. But you could have handled my emotions better?"

"Can't you just calm down, so we can talk? I'm trying to apologize here."

"You know what you can do with your apology? Shove it up your ass on the way out of my house."

Richard turns toward Jacob with a look and gesture that clearly reads as 'see what I mean.' Jacob says nothing, but his look is one of pure disgust. I couldn't love him more than I do at this moment. Without a word, he validates me in front of Richard. For so long, Richard had made me think I was crazy, that I was the one imagining things. He was a big part of why the depression had pulled me so far under and lasted for so long. He had no empathy, couldn't have cared at all that I'd suffered two big losses close together. He'd never even taken the time to find out why I was estranged from my grandmother or what my childhood had been like. Ten years together, and he'd never really cared about me as a person.

"The lady asked you to leave, so I think it's time you go," Jacob says, his voice broaching no argument.

"We're not done here," Richard says, turning back in my direction, arrogance etched into every line of his forehead.

"We've been done for a long time, Richard, and there's no need for you to be here."

I will not let him get the upper hand. As if reading the determination on my face, he lifts the envelope he'd quietly set on the island in front of himself. A snide smile crosses his face, and my chest constricts. What's he up to?

"In this envelope are two sets of divorce papers drawn up by my lawyer. We can talk and sign the one more agreeable to both of us, or you can continue this farce of fortitude, and the only one I'll be signing is the one that benefits me."

Jacob's nostrils flare as he pushes off the doorway. I slightly shake my head, catching Richard's smirk at the movement. He's goading me, goading us both. But to what end? What is he getting from being here.

"I'm listening. Since you obviously could have sent the copy you wanted me to sign here, there's a reason for your presence. What is it?"

"Nice house you've got here," Richard says, looking around the newly restored kitchen. "Why did we never visit during our marriage?"

My hackles rise. I know Richard doesn't really care, nor would he have wanted to come here. "Much like the home we shared, I have many not-so-happy memories here."

A dark look crosses Richard's face before he restores the snide smile. "Oh, so I'm surprised you decided to come back here, yet you wouldn't come back home."

"You asked me for the divorce, Richard. You made that decision."

A bright smile spreads across his face, and he relaxes at the same time Jacob stiffens. What is happening? Jacob's anger and discomfort at the turn in the conversation is understandable, but Richard's shift in demeanor doesn't make much sense. I don't trust him, and if he's happy, something is definitely wrong.

"You should've tried to come back, Morgan. I'd have taken you back if you'd have asked. You could still ask."

Richard's voice takes on a hopeful tone, saccharine sweet, and he reaches out to grasp my hand. I have to steel myself from immediately yanking it away. I still need to figure out his game. What is he after?

"I'm not going back, Richard."

His lips draw into a straight line while his back stiffens. "You can't say you haven't missed me, Morgan. We were together for nearly more than a decade."

"And you walked away. In fact, you threw it in my face. You were having an affair. Why would I want to go back to that?"

"You were despondent. You were unresponsive. You were ignoring me."

"I was fucking depressed. I had just lost my mother. You were so worried about yourself, you never even tried to comfort me."

His nostrils flare, and his voice rises. "You used me to get away from her. Why the hell would I comfort you at her loss?"

"You're such an ass. Get to your point, and get the fuck out of my grandmother's house!" My hands are shaking at this point, and I can hardly control the urge to slap him across the face. I have no doubt Jacob would protect me from any retaliation, but I don't want to put him in that position.

"Here is the point, Morgan. You walked out on our marriage long before I asked you to leave. I want my ring back."

Incredulity flows through me in waves, and I barely stifle a laugh. "Your ring? Do you mean the ring that I have been wearing for all these years. The ring that was supposedly a promise to hold and cherish in good or bad? That ring? The one you ignored when you stepped out with someone else?"

"I want the ring, Morgan. I bought it. It's mine. Everything I bought is mine. By rights, I bought you, and you're mine." He bangs his fist on the table.

"Pull out those fucking divorce papers, Richard. You can eat the fucking ring for all I care, and I hope you fucking choke on it!"

I stand, shoving the barstool back so roughly it hits against the counter behind me. I walk out of the room, pass Jacob without a word, and head up the stairs to the bedroom. Getting on my knees, I dig through the bottom of the armoire. *Fuck these old houses and their lack of real closets! Fuck men lacking hearts!* The familiar sting burns the backs of my eyes. *Fuck crying over a marriage that should never have been. Fuck him seeing my tears. Richard Dartmouth could fuck right the fuck off!* Even after all these years, I can barely bring myself to say the word fuck, let alone directly to someone, but damn if Richard doesn't have me throwing it around like confetti, even in my own head. . Swiping at the lone tear hanging in the corner of my eye, I make my way back downstairs, my hand tightly closed around the ring I only stopped wearing the morning I'd decided to come home.

CHAPTER TWENTY

I'LL SHOW YOU OUT

*J*acob

We're still where she left us when she returns to the kitchen. My eyes bore holes into the back of Richard's head where the prick is leaned back with his feet crossed at the ankles like he's enjoying a cup of coffee on a veranda somewhere and not sucking up all the air Morgan has managed to breathe back into this old house. As it is, I keep picturing him buried under the back porch. Unfortunately, I've already completed that project and would have to reopen the floor, not that I'm against the idea.

Morgan returns to the kitchen and takes her seat at the island again. She looks at the two nearly identical stacks of paper and raises an eyebrow at Richard who simply tilts his head in a gesture that tells her to look over the documents. She picks up the first stack and silently skims through the pages. I watch her face closely and catch the silent scoff before she says anything.

"Irreconcilable differences?" Her tone is flat, but her next words are pointed. "You were having an affair during my greatest time of need. There's nothing to reconcile."

I start to chuckle, but her brows pinch together in confusion and then consternation. Something in those papers has her rankled, and my hands ball into fists. I know she doesn't want me to do anything to the man, but I'll be damned if I'm going to just stand here and let this asshole hurt her again. When her face blanches, I inch closer to her from behind Richard, but she holds up a hand for me to stay put.

"You really are a heartless bastard, Richard," she finally says, and my stomach tightens at the disgust in her voice. I don't have to read the document to know that it must threaten to take something important from her. The only thing it could be, unless she owns something else I don't know about, is this house. That realization has me wanting to wrap my hands around the scumbag's throat.

For his part, Richard doesn't argue, which is smart of him because I might not be able to hold myself back if he says something of the cuff. Morgan picks up the other packet and lays the pages side-by-side. Her eyes travel back and forth between the piles, and her nostrils flare. She takes a couple of deep breaths before looking up at Richard.

"I see you're much more amenable to the second version," Richard says, sitting up straight, his voice condescending.

"And how can I trust that you won't do something shady like transfer my signature to that other copy." I'm wondering the same thing.

He shrugs. "If I wanted to forge your signature, Morgan, I'd have done it already. I wanted my ring back, and you would not answer my calls. Do you think I wanted to come out to this godforsaken mudpit of a town?" He scoffs. "I'll sign first if that makes you feel better. Do you have a copy machine here? You can make a copy."

She looks at the papers strewn all over the table. "No. I don't have one here yet," she says quietly, putting the piles back together. Her eyes shine with unshed tears, and I want to wrap her up in my arms.

"My sister has one at the store," I interject to take the pressure off of her. "On top of owning the store, she's also a notary and can notarized the signatures to bear witness that you're signing the one you agree to."

"Ah, that would explain her reticence to give me any information. She's your sister," Richard says with a sneer. "We can go back to that store and sign there if you prefer, Morgan, or you can give me my ring, we sign now, and you're rid of me."

A snort slips from her at his ridiculous offer, and the corner of my lip tilts up. He may not realize it, but she will be rid of him regardless. I'll make sure of it.

"We'll meet you at the store," Morgan says. "I assume you can find your way back there." She turns her attention to me. "Do you mind driving me? I can get Joanna to bring me back, so you don't have to make a second trip."

My brows draw together. I hope she knows that I'll do anything she asks. I open my mouth to tell her so, but she tips her head to the side, and her eyes give me a pleading look. I just stare at her trying to decipher the expression. It takes a moment before I shake my head, clearing the confusion, and pull out my keys. Nothing more needs to be said.

"Let me grab my purse," she says, grabbing one of the packets, presumably the unwanted copy of the divorce papers from the table, and making her way upstairs. It's a smart way to make sure Richard doesn't switch out anything before they sign them at the store. I don't know the man, but from Morgan's response to the document she has clutched to her chest when she leaves the room, I wouldn't put it past him to pull some bullshit like that.

"I'll show you out," I say as she gets to the landing and enters her room.

CHAPTER TWENTY-ONE

HEARTBREAKS AND HAPPINESS

Morgan

I seethe the entire ride over to the hardware store. Jacob must feel my anger because he says nothing and just lets me stew in it. Thankfully, he also doesn't ask any questions. He already looked ready to take Richard outside from the moment the asshole stepped foot across the threshold of my house. If he knew what the document said, he might still actually do it. Still, it's hard to believe that our ten-year marriage was reduced to two piles of papers. One that completely ruined me if I dare step out of line, and the other that provides the bare minimum for playing along.

I might not have understood all the legalese used in the divorce papers, and Lord knows I can't afford a lawyer, but I knew there was nothing good in Richard's sudden appearance in Colliers Town. In the copy currently hidden in the bottom of my wardrobe, right where I'd kept the ring that's burning a hole in my pocket, Richard had tried to take everything from me. Not only would I not get a cent in the settlement, which doesn't matter because I want nothing from him, but he would get half of my grandmother's house. It said the house would be sold at auction, and we'd split the proceeds. The house that I've been pouring myself into to restore. The house that is all I have left in the world of my family. The house that is the only thing keeping me from being homeless.

Joanna is cordial throughout the whole process, but I can feel the animosity emanating in the space between her and Jacob. Somehow, their anger on my behalf makes this whole situation bearable. I don't think I've ever had anyone on my side, truly standing beside me, and it feels good. It feels like home.

When Richard finally leaves, and I'm able to breathe again, Jacob agrees to go check on their father while Joanna finishes closing up the shop. We'll meet at the bar down the street for dinner and a couple drinks to celebrate.

"Thanks so much for serving as our notary, J. I really appreciate it."

"Of course. If I hadn't known who he was, I'd have thought your ex was a nice-looking guy."

"He is nice looking, even as he's gotten older, but he can be a real dick. He came here to threaten to take my house if I didn't give him my ring back."

"He did what? I should have taken a shovel to the back of his head!"

I laugh and hug her as we walk out the door. It truly is remarkable how quickly we've picked up our relationship and returned to the same level of closeness and understanding from before I left all those years ago. Joanna knows the right things to say to cut the tension I'm holding, and she's willing to do whatever is needed. I hate that we've lost so many years because of insecurities and misunderstandings.

"I'm so glad you were still here when I came back to town. I don't know if I would have made it through these past couple of months without you. Hell, I don't know if I would have been able to make it through today as unscathed as I have without both you and Jacob. You for the warning, and him for the silent support."

Joanna smiles but it quickly falters.

"What's wrong?" I ask, grabbing her arm.

She shakes her head. "Nothing. I'm really glad you and Jake have found each other again. I knew he would be there this morning, and thankfully, I wasn't wrong."

"Um, J, you look anything but happy. Talk to me."

Joanna sniffles and pulls me forward down the sidewalk. "Let's get a booth in the back, and then I'll see if I can make it quick and sweet before Jake joins us."

I don't like the sound of her tone. Joanna rarely keeps anything from her brother. They are twins after all. What could possibly be so wrong that she's not only near tears but that she also doesn't want him to know about it. As soon as we find a table at the bar, we order a round of drinks.

"Ok, spill it," I say, unable to wait any longer.

With a heavy sigh, she looks into my eyes. "Do you remember the guy I hung out with at the stage during the Fall Festival?" I nod and gesture for her to continue. "Well, we hooked up later that night."

"What?" My outburst catches the attention of the other patrons in the area, and I lower my voice again. "You did what? Why didn't you tell me?"

"I wanted to. I tried to. My brother was just always around. This was not something I wanted to tell him, especially not after the way he acted when he'd met the guy that night."

I can understand her reluctance. Jacob had been a bit of a dick about the guy hanging out with her.

"So, tell me all about it, and make it quick! I want details, woman."

Joanna explains that she had given him her number earlier before Jacob and I returned from the hayride. She hadn't expected him to call her, but he'd sent a text that very night. Apparently, they'd spent a couple hours sexting and agreed to meet up halfway between Colliers Town and the cabin he and his friends were staying at on the other side of the lake. They'd spent the night and next morning in a hotel room. He told her about his life in New York, and they both shared their plans for the future.

"How was the sex, though?"

"Girl, he was experienced, much more experienced than me. He did things to my body I had only read about in books, and it was oh so good. But then he was gone."

"What do you mean gone?" My brows draw together. I don't want to have to find this guy and chop off his balls.

"He didn't sneak off on me or anything like that. I simply meant that the experience was life changing for me, and he just went back to his life like nothing happened."

I jump to her side of the booth and plop down, putting my arms around her. I know that feeling well and hate that she's feeling this pain.

"It can be devastating when an experience doesn't have the same effect on others that it does on you. I can see it's still bothering you."

"What's bothering you, sis?" Jacob asks as he slides into the booth I had vacated mere moments before.

I quickly close my eyes, torn between wishing he had waited a few minutes longer and glad to see him. Even after all these years, just looking at him makes my stomach quiver.

"Nothing, Jake. I'm good."

He looks at her incredulously, and I slip back to his side of the booth, hoping to distract him from bothering his sister. When he doesn't take his eyes off of Joanna, I climb into his lap, straddling him. Thank goodness this place has tables that move in their booths, or I wouldn't have been able to squeeze myself in here with him. Joanna giggles behind me as the table locks her into her seat.

"Do you know what today is, Jacob Daniels?"

He looks up, his gaze heated. I nip at his lower lip that's pouted out. Before I can answer my own question, he claims my mouth and wraps his arms around my waist, pulling me tightly against him.

"Ugh, get a room, you two," Joanna says.

There's mirth in her tone and I'm happy to see her feeling better after our talk. There's still more to say, but now isn't the time. I'll find a way to get some time alone with Joanna, even if I have to go hang out at the store Monday morning while Jacob's at work. I look down into his eyes and then kiss the tip of his nose before climbing off him and turning to face Joanna, my legs across Jacob's lap.

"Today, I am officially a free woman and able to make all of my own decisions..." My voice hitches, and I have to take a deep breath before I can continue. "For the first time in my entire fucking life."

"This calls for a celebration," Jacob says with a huge grin as he waves for the server.

The three of us enjoy each other's company, taking shots and chasing them down with various mixed drinks until we're all completely shitfaced.

"I haven't been this drunk in ages," I admit.

"Me either," Joanna says, looking toward the door like it's miles away.

"I think we might need to call for a ride," Jacob offers. "None of us are in any condition to drive, and we all live too far away to walk."

CHAPTER TWENTY-TWO

DON'T CHANGE YOUR MIND

*M*organ

Less than an hour later, the twins' dad picks us up in the same old mustang he's had since we were kids.

"Thanks, Mr. Daniels. I'm so sorry we had to get you out of the house."

"It's fine. Contrary to public belief thanks to my overprotective children, I am not an invalid, nor am I a recluse." His voice is gravelly but soft.

I turn to look at him from where I'm seated in the front seat of the car. I remember him being super intimidating when I was younger. He looks far less scary now, like the years have mellowed him out or maybe it's just that I've seen a lot worse since then.

"They told me they took turns caring for you," I say, my voice slurring no matter how hard I'm trying to keep it steady.

Joanna and Jacob are in the back seat, heads leaned together. They're either both asleep or passed out, not that there's much difference. Mr. Daniels looks in the rearview mirror, observing them.

"What they're doing is taking turns coddling me." Though his voice is gruffer this time, there's no animosity in it. His tone is playful, like he finds their behavior amusing. "Sorry. When their mother passed away a few years back, I had a really hard time. She had been the love of my life, and I couldn't imagine a life without her."

He's gripping the steering wheel so tightly, his knuckles are white. I reach over and pat his hand reassuringly.

"You don't have to explain yourself to me, Mr. Daniels."

"My son loves you, you know," he says abruptly. I gasp, and he glances at me quickly before turning his eyes back to the dark road. "He always has. Ever since before you left town and never returned. He pined for you, waited for you, put his entire life on hold for you. I guess I did the same when I lost my Rosie."

Whether from the alcohol, his story of loss, or my own emotions, I can't stop the tears from falling. They blaze trails down my face, and my breath hitches.

"Truth be told, Ms. Humphries..."

"Please call me Morgan."

"Morgan," he says, his voice softer than it had been, "I wish we, as a town, had done a better job of protecting you, of making you feel welcome. I can't imagine it was easy to come back here."

"Joanna and Jacob have made my return bearable. I don't know what I would have done without them as a kid, and I don't know what I would have done without them when I came back."

"We have that in common then. I don't know what I would have done without them either, but ..." he trails off.

I look out into the darkness as we drive toward their family home. It's been ages since I've been to this side of town. My grandmother hadn't let me go to their house too often because of Jacob, even before I'd been interested in him as more than just my best friend's brother who played pranks on us. The few times I did make it out to their homestead, I'd been fascinated by the pastures and animals. I can't help but wonder who's been taking care of the animals all this time if he hasn't been able to do much, especially since both Joanna and Jacob have jobs outside the home? I'm honestly not sure I want to know. If the two wonderful people in the back seat have had those responsibilities and still manage to spend so much time helping me, the guilt will eat me alive. It's bad enough I never thought to ask. When we pull into the driveway, I turn back to look at him. He looks tired and gaunt, not nearly the man he had been when I was a child.

"Do you all still have the animals? I loved coming to see them the few times my grandmother would let me out here." He clears his throat, and I looked up toward his eyes. They're sparkling, and I have the sneaky suspicion he's on the verge of tears. "Mr. Daniels? Are you alright?"

He sniffs and clears his throat again. "Yes. Yes, I'm okay. I rarely leave because coming home is hard. My Rosie would always be at the door waiting for me, no matter my reason for leaving or the time I returned." He takes a deep breath, and I reach out to squeeze his hand again. "We have a few animals left, mainly chickens and Jacob's horse. He's old now, so no one rides him anymore. He's kind of like me, just sitting around waiting for it all to end."

I shake my head hard, though he doesn't look in my direction. His grief breaks my heart. "Maybe you both are just waiting for someone to come along and remind you that you're still alive. I know what it feels like to forget and to move through a fog, but the end isn't the only ending. You know?"

He turns his hand over and squeezes mine back. "Thank you."

He parks the car in front of the house, and we both get out. I stumble a bit before catching myself. Then I open the back door, grab at the closest shoulder, and shake it.

"J, wake up." Joanna doesn't move, just snuggles her head onto her brother's shoulder more. "Joanna, let's go in the house."

"Jacob, get your drunk ass up, boy," their father says with so much authority, all three of us jump.

"Dad?" Both Jacob and Joanna say at the same time.

"Get out the car and in the house, you two. Morgan is barely holding herself upright over there, and my old ass is tired after coming to pick you all up. Didn't think I'd have to play DD to my 35-year-old children."

I look over the top of the car at him, and there's a huge grin on his face. I snort, trying to hold in my laughter. He looks up and winks.

"Morgana," Jacob says, "are you okay?"

"She'd be fine if you two didn't have her standing outside here. All of you need to sleep it off, but I doubt you want to do that in the car."

"Yessir," Jacob responds, shuffling his way out of the backseat, holding onto the car door as he stands.

Jacob looks around, and when his eyes land on me, he smiles. I'm still feeling tipsy, but it's obvious Jacob is far beyond that. I again have to stifle a giggle when Joanna crawls, literally, crawls her way out of the car, almost face planting into the dirt. I nearly tumble with her when I try to stop her fall.

"You okay, J?" I ask.

"I think I'm going to be sick," Joanna responds.

I take a step back from her, and Mr. Daniels comes around the car to grab his daughter around the shoulders.

"Would serve you right," he says, leading her into the house.

His voice holds none of the scolding his words promise, and I decide then and there that I like him. Even if he was harsh and formidable in my childhood, I like the man he is now. By the time Mr. Daniels gets Joanna into the house, Jacob has made his way around the car to me.

"Hey there, my beautiful witch. You got me drunk."

"You got yourself drunk, Jacob Daniels. We were supposed to be celebrating my freedom, and I think you celebrated more than I did."

"I may be just a little happier than you."

I scoff and go to playfully slap his shoulder, but I miss and almost trip over my own feet.

"Whoa, Morgana. Not so light on your feet there."

He wraps his arms around me and places a quick kiss on my lips. I love the feel of his lips on mine and his hands clutching my hips. I run my hands up his chest and around his neck to pull his mouth back to mine. When our tongues touch, I moan and melt into him. His body is so warm, and mine is warming from the inside out with his kiss.

"Are you two coming inside, or am I locking you outside to sleep in the barn?"

Jacob breaks the kiss off and leans his forehead against mine with a laugh. "I guess we better go inside."

"Can you even walk straight?"

"I was able to make your eyes cross just now, so I think I'm good," he says, laughing harder when I lean up and bite his bottom lip. "You already have me at your mercy, Morgana, you don't need my blood for one of your magic spells."

"Shut up," I say and turn toward the porch. "We're coming," I yell up to Mr. Daniels.

When I turn back around, Jacob pulls me into his arms and stares down at me. I give him a small smile and raise a questioning brow.

"Do you remember our first night together after you came home?" He asks after a few seconds. I nod but don't say a word. "That next morning, you told me we didn't know each other enough to just pick up where we left off 20 years ago." I swallow down the lump forming in my throat. He just smiles. "I reintroduced myself and made you a promise. Do you remember what it was?"

Tears prick the backs of my eyes from the way love pours from him. It's unwavering, and I can't believe I nearly walked away from him completely for the second time.

"You said you were going to marry me."

"I did say that. I fucked up tonight and let the celebration get away from me, but I had a plan when I walked into that bar."

I tilt my head at him. And when he drops to one knee, I gasp, covering my mouth with my hand like a cliche.

"I know it may seem ironic, maybe even selfish, to ask you to give up your newly reclaimed singlehood, but you own every piece of my heart. You bewitched me the first time you came to Colliers Town for the summer, and you stole my heart piece by piece every time you left. I feel whole for the first time in 20 years, and I'm afraid to wait any longer." Unable to speak, I hold my breath as a single tear runs down my cheek. "Morgana, the only woman I've ever loved, will you marry me?"

I stare at him, my nostrils flaring from all of the emotions. I can't even make sense of them. Slowly, I take in a deep breath and let it out. He stares back, anticipation written on his face. I hope he isn't still drunk because it would really suck to wake up in the morning and find he didn't mean any of it.

"What, no ring?" I ask with a light chuckle.

His brows furrow for a second, and then he laughs. "Oh, yeah, that." He stands and reaches into the front pocket of his jeans. When he pulls out a black, velvet box, the tears stream down my cheeks freely. He stops laughing. "I can put it away and try again later. I mean it, Morgana, you are it for me, so if it's too soon, I will wait."

I watch him blink multiple times as he cups the box tightly in his hands, hiding it from view. Before he can put it back in his pocket, though, I put my hands on his.

"If you give that to me, Jacob Daniels, I promise you will never get it back. So be sure about this because I will not survive you changing your mind afterwards. Not you."

"Is that a yes?"

"Yes, boy!" his dad yells from the porch. "Though you really could have just slept in the same room without all the pomp and circumstance in the middle of the driveway."

He ignores his father's jab. "Morgana," he says quietly, the question held between us.

"I don't ever want to imagine a life without you again, Jacob Daniels. It's a yes," I say with a series of nods, like my body insists on punctuating my answer.

"Really?" he asks with an excited exhalation of breath.

"If you don't put that ring on my finger and take me to bed," I whisper-yell, so his father won't hear me and add another unwanted two cents.

Jacob smiles, opens the box, and slips the sapphire and diamond ring on my finger. I gasp when the stone catches the porch light, showing its deep blue depths.

"It reminded me of your eyes."

I wrap my arms around his neck and pull him down for a kiss that hopefully conveys everything I feel in this moment. When we pulled apart, Jacob leads me up the porch steps, and Mr. Daniels wraps us both in a tight hug.

"Finally," Joanna's chimes in from where she stands inside the screen door before she steps out onto the porch and wraps herself around all of us.

CHAPTER TWENTY-THREE

SHOW ME HOW GOOD

*J*acob

I wake with the sun. There is nothing more beautiful than watching the sunlight play across Morgan's face while she still sleeps. Soon, she'll have this house all ready, and I'll have to share her with others, meaning she'll be up way before sunrise. As much as I hate the idea of not having her to myself every day, I can't wait to see how successful this place becomes.

We've switched out the twin-size bed that was in this room for a queen. Not only will it be a much better size for guests, but it's damn sure much more comfortable. Not going to lie, though, I can't wait for her to work up the courage to go through Gretna Humphries' suite. The things I will do to this woman in a king-size bed will likely get me kicked out of church. Oh wait, I don't go anymore.

"Good morning, sunshine," she says without opening her eyes, and I can't help but smile. It's like she can read my mind and know when I'm rambling to myself.

"Good morning, enchantress." I kiss her nose before running my own down her jawline to her collar bone. She reaches up a hand and runs it through my hair. I continue my descent, peppering kisses along her shoulder and over the swell of her breasts. My hand slides up between them, and I grab her chin, tilting her head down to look at me.

Her areolas are a dark, dusty pink, and just the sight of them has my mouth watering. When she finally opens her eyes, I lock my gaze with hers and pull one of her nipples into my mouth. Her lips part, and I let my teeth graze the nipple, causing her to suck in a breath. I repeat the action with the other, and she lets out a moan.

"Are you hungry?" she asks, and I smile against her. "I mean, would you like me to make you some breakfast."

She's so cute when she's playing coy. Though she's not naive or inexperienced, I've learned that her personal experience before, with, and since that prick of an ex-husband was seriously lacking. Now, it's not only my mission to make sure she's the happiest she's ever been, but it's also imperative I make sure she's more satisfied than she knew was possible.

"You have everything I need right here," I say and continue kissing a trail over her belly. Instinctively, she opens her legs for me to slide down between them. She's bare from last night's lovemaking, and I can't wait until I have her sleeping nude every night. The past couple months have been a whirlwind of busyness between my construction business and helping her with remodeling the house that we've only talked about me moving in, not actually acted on it. Another reason I hope she'll soon be willing to empty out that private suite downstairs. We can't both comfortably fit with our things in this small room. Not that I don't spend nearly every night in this bed by her side, and between these legs.

"You're so fucking beautiful, Morgana," I say, kissing her inner thighs between each word. "I will never get enough of you." I slide my hands up those same deliciously thick thighs and spread her open. She glistens with arousal, and I find myself breathing her in again. "All these months, and I still can't believe you're here and you're mine."

She whimpers when I place a kiss on her clit and do nothing more than hold my lips there. "Jacob, please."

"Hmmm," I intone on a chuckle, letting my mouth vibrate against her. I could prolong the torture, but the smell of her is entirely too delicious to not indulge. "Maybe I am hungry after all." With those words, I flatten my tongue against her, licking from her opening to her clit before flicking it with the tip.

"God," flies out of her mouth, and I smile before wrapping my lips around her clit and sucking it into my mouth. "Holy fuck! Jacob. Yes." Morgan rarely cusses. It's just not part of her everyday vocabulary, but here, beneath me, her responses let me know how close she is to coming undone. This morning won't take long at all from the sound of it.

Her thighs clench around my neck, holding me close, and I don't try to pull away. Instead, I dive in, licking and sucking until she's panting, and I'm snarling like a dog with a bone. She is the sweetest treat, and I would not want to be held accountable for what might happen to anyone who tried to interrupt us right now.

"Shit," she screeches. I take my mouth off of her just for a second to wet my fingers before taking her clit back between my lips. Then, I slide two fingers inside her wet pussy. I could easily slide my dick inside her right now, but I want her levitating off the bed, coming all over my face and hand. "Fuck, Jacob. Don't stop," she says when I start working my fingers inside of her. My hand is already soaked from her arousal, and the sound of her wetness has my dick leaking. "Oh my God," she cries out as she clenches around my fingers and lifts her hips from the bed.

"There it is," I say when I lift my mouth from her and get up on my knees to pound my fingers in and out of her, feeling the moment she releases completely and squirts all over me and the bed. She screams my name, and I revel in the sound, primal noises coming from me as I work her all the way through her release.

Her eyelids start to droop, but I'm not done yet. I move back between her legs and notch my swollen tip at her entrance. She opens her eyes and bites her bottom lip. The post-orgasmic glow lights up her face, and she moans, lifting her hips to meet mine as I plunge into her. She wraps around me perfectly, like she was created to mold to my dick. When I'm fully seated, she puts her ankles up on my shoulders and rocks her hips up and down, fucking me. Each upward move squeezes me tight, and it takes all my strength not to come from the sensation and the sounds of her wet pussy taking me. Not yet though. I want to pull another orgasm from her body before I fill her.

"Who's fucking who?" I ask with a smile on my face, and she looks up at me with a sly smirk. In the same breath, I feel her walls tighten as she slows her rocking. "That's it, Morgana, fuck me." I know she's trying to make me come, but I'm not ready. I want to feel her pulsating... My thoughts break off when she starts winding her hips in circles as she draws me in and out of her. "Fuuuuck." My eyes roll back, and I grit my teeth. "You feel so good," I barely get out around the moans she's pulling from me. She really is a sorceress.

"Show me how good," is all she says, and it's all over for me.

I yell out my release, wrapping my arms around her legs to hold myself upright. "Damn," is the only word that comes from my mouth once I catch my breath. I kiss the insides of each of her ankles before letting myself slide over to the side, not letting go of her legs or pulling out completely. Nothing feels better than being inside of my Morgana, so I never rush to let her go.

"You okay over there?" She giggles from my side.

"Sometimes I wonder if you aren't trying to kill me."

She blows air from her nose like she's trying to hold in another laugh, and I turn my head to look at her. Her body is turned toward me out of necessity, considering I'm still holding her legs up over my chest. The glint of amusement in her eyes makes me smile.

"Now why would I want to do a thing like that and lose access to..." she trails off, gesturing at me from head to toe. "All this."

"It's all yours to do with as you will," I say before pulling out and kissing her nose. "Now that you've had it, how about we get this day started? There's work to be done, unless you've figured out how to work some magic and finish it all up with a wriggle of that cute nose of yours."

She lets out a groan and slaps her hands down on the bed. "Fine."

CHAPTER TWENTY-FOUR

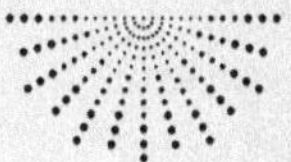

A COUPLE BIRDIES SENT ME

*M*organ

A car pulls up to the house. I thought I was imagining it at first because no one is supposed to be coming by this early. Closing my laptop, I make my way to the window for a quick peek before I open the door. Surprise has me striding toward the entry, and my eyes grow wide when the man steps out of the familiar mustang.

"Mr. Daniels? What're you doing here?"

Garrett Daniels raises his eyes to mine, and a smile lights up his face. Without a word, he leans back into the car and pulls something out of the backseat. Closing the door, he turns back toward me and slings whatever he'd grabbed over his shoulder. His smile is still set firmly in place, and I can't help but smile back, though I'm sure confusion is written in my brows.

"A couple of birdies," he says, his low timbre traversing the space, "told me that you were closing in on the opening of a new business and needed a daytime handyman to help finish up the odd jobs that aren't done."

I stand on the porch stunned. Neither Jacob nor Joanna mentioned anything about sending their father to help. Hell, they both still act like he's an invalid most days. He's definitely not, and as he approaches, I can tell that he doesn't think so either. The thing he has slung over his shoulder is a tool belt.

"You know what, I do have a couple small jobs. How are your locksmith skills?"

"Am I picking the lock or changing it?"

I laugh. "Maybe just taking down the whole damn door."

"Oh, I am good at demolition!"

"Where were you months ago?"

"Wallowing in the pits of despair where my children left me."

"Well, Mr. Daniels, it is good to see you back on Earth."

"Thank you for giving them something else to focus on, so I could focus on me for a while."

Without thinking about it, I wrap my arms around his waist in a tight hug. I still can't believe I had been so intimidated by this man as a child. He's nothing like I imagined him to be. Then again, I'm no longer the person I was back then either. That thought has me smiling as I lead him into the house.

"How about a grand tour?" I offer as we cross the threshold. He takes a moment to look around the entry that is still much darker than I want it to be, even in the middle of the day. After a few seconds, he gestures for me to lead the way.

*M*organ

I pause the sandwich halfway to my lips when I hear Garrett's bellowed "Son of a bitch," from the first-floor suite. The first task I gave him was to change all the locks my grandmother had put up throughout her suite. It's not that I'm ready to go through her things, but I don't want the skeleton keys to be the reason I can't sweep out the skeletons from her closet.

Besides, I only have a couple months left to move out of that upstairs room, so it's ready for guests.

Letting the sandwich fall back onto the plate, I quickly make my way to where Garrett is kneeling in front of the bedroom door holding one hand in the other. "Oh my God, are you alright?" His breathing is heavy, and I can't tell if it's from pain or frustration.

"I was pretty sure you were kidding when you said you might be removing doors, but this one here might actually have to go. I think your grandmother's ghost is trying to kill me."

I want to chuckle at his dramatic words, but his tone is serious. Strewn around him are screwdrivers of various sizes, the box of keys I'd given him earlier, a hammer and a chisel, as well as a pry bar. What in the world?

He must catch sight of my confused look because he lets out an exaggerated sigh. "I've tried everything I know to remove this lock, but the safety plate here will not come off, so I can't change out the handle or the locking mechanism. I've removed the screws, tried getting under it with the chisel, and even tried prying off the handle. Nothing fucking works." Then he holds up his hand, and there's blood dripping down the side. "And now I've cut my damn self when the pry bar slipped."

"Oh no! Let me see," I say, reaching out for his hand.

He shakes his head. "I'll be fine. I'm just pissed that this damn door bested me."

"Stay there," I admonish when he goes to stand. "I'll go get the first aid kit." Thankfully, I had remembered to ask Joanna to bring me one a few weeks ago. If not, he'd be stuck with Grandma Gretna's old mercurochrome.

After I get him cleaned up, I return to my lunch that I no longer want. Not only do I hate that Garrett's hurt himself already on his first day out of the house, but standing in the doorway of Grandma Gretna's bedroom has me feeling like the ghosts of my past are circling around. Garrett's comment about my grandmother's ghost working to keep him from removing the lock from the bedroom door hasn't helped the feeling any. Maybe I'm just meant to keep that part of the house closed to everyone.

"Don't worry. When Jake gets here, we'll just take down that door and put up a new one. Maybe we'll..."

I don't let him finish the statement. "It can wait. There are other things that can be worked on in the meantime, and maybe we'll just move the door to the end of the hallway, making that area the business office and off-limits to guests." He just nods and begins picking up the tools and tucking them back into his tool belt. "In the meantime, I'll just focus on hiring an assistant."

CHAPTER TWENTY-FIVE

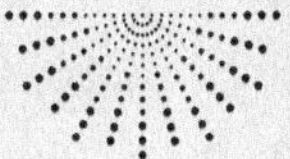

PART OF THE PACKAGE

*M*organ

My lungs tighten as I try to breathe through the panic. I've barely opened the website and scheduled the open house last week, and yet I'm fully booked for Spring Break. I wasn't even sure I'd get people interested for the season because Colliers Town is a little further from the lake than some other bed and breakfast places in the county. So, I couldn't even conceive of this level of support. Hopefully, today will be the day I find an assistant, so I can focus on other last-minute items, like setting the menu for the open house that will take place in two weeks.

Colliers Town is growing. It had already started making the first steps before I'd come back home, but I see it happening. Plans are being made to expand the major highway that normally takes people south of Cole County. Now, it'll have a major thoroughfare linking the interstate to the lake and the mountains on this side, rather than just through Carruthersville. Hopefully, Colliers Town won't grow into a city, even a small city, but I can't wait to see how we can grow and modernize while still keeping the small-town feel. The biggest boon wouldn't just be to the economy; it would also help keep some of the younger folk around. Now that I'm back, I don't want to see it become a sleepy town where everyone escapes as soon as they can. I came back, and I want to make sure others have something to come back to.

It's hard to believe I only started cleaning out the house eight months ago, and now it's finally returning to my great grandmother's original plan. Though it won't be a rooming house for men working the mines, like what was needed at the turn of the previous century, there will be people staying in the home. I can't wait. The ground floor has been completely repainted and Jacob helped convert it into a true showcase with a library, sitting room, small workspace with ethernet connection for business travelers, and the now not-so-formal dining room. We took the heavy royal table out of the huge space and repurposed to wood to make smaller, more intimate seating options. There are a couple of high bars along the wall with internet hookups and plugs, so those who want to eat but need to work can do both. There's also a partition between the communal seating that includes 8-people tables with stools that can be used by multiple parties, and two quiet tables for 2-4 people who are there to share a more intimate time together.

A small voice pulls me from my thoughts. "Hello? I'm here about the job."

"Back here. Come straight down the hall and into the kitchen."

Though I've created other spaces more appropriate for business meetings and interviews, I still prefer to do business in the kitchen. Until the house is bustling with people and needing enough staff to make the kitchen inaccessible, I plan to continue using it.

"Welcome," I say, standing and holding out my hand.

The woman standing in the doorway is young, maybe early 20s. She has soft brown hair with hints of pink streaks that are curled at the ends, so it bounces as she comes into the room. Though her voice sounds a bit uncertain, her green eyes show strength and a hint of defiance. She's dressed simply enough in a pair of powder-blue slacks and a pinstripe button-down shirt that's tucked into her unbelted waistband. She has on chunky-soled, cow-print shoes, and she's carrying an extra-large bag with a huge 3D magnolia blossom on the side. She exudes creativity and exuberance, two things I really want in this house.

I smile and invite her to take a seat at the island that is easily my favorite piece of furniture in the house. Of course, Jacob made it for me, but really, I love it because it's exactly what I'd envisioned in this space. It was the first change I'd mentioned when I moved in, and he'd built and installed it that next month. After our initial introductions, I offer Taylor a cup of coffee.

"No thanks. I'm not a fan." Her wan smile says she's waiting for some question or statement about that preference. She'll never get that from me.

"I can't stand the stuff either, but I know we'll be throwing away any chance at success if we don't serve it."

Her smile widens. "Coffee lovers are like a cult and can't believe there are people out here who might be disgusted by the taste or even the smell."

I watch Taylor for a few moments, deciding I already like her, before asking the basic interview questions. I'd been wrong about her age. She'll turn twenty-six at the end of April. In fact, she's the eldest of four and has experience in hospitality and restaurants. Her clothes alone make her stand out, but she exudes positive energy, though some sadness shines in her eyes when she talks about her siblings.

"Now for the most important question," I say. "Why are you here in Colliers Town? You're obviously not from here, and most of our young people are looking to get away."

Taylor clasps her hands and takes a deep breath before speaking. "I hate to say that I'm running away from responsibility at twenty-five, but I had to get away. I had to move far enough away to find myself and reconnect with the parts of me that were withering, and yet I didn't want to be too far from my siblings. My stepdad just...well...let's just say, I had to leave."

I struggle to keep my eyes as neutral as possible as my brain fills in the spaces Taylor leaves in her story, and I nod with as empathetic a smile as I can. Taylor takes another steadying breath and inclines her head. To change the subject and break the tension, I stand.

"Let me show you around," I say, leading Taylor out of the kitchen and up the stairs.

Organ

Close to an hour later, we make our way down the hall toward the kitchen. Our laughter spreads throughout the empty space, echoing in my ears. There's been more laughter in this house these past seven months than there were the entire ten years I'd come to visit my grandmother. I haven't told Taylor yet, but I've already decided to hire her. She has a keen eye for details and some wonderful ideas to make the house more inviting, so people will want to come stay. I have no doubt they'll want to return after being here.

"What's down that short hall there?" Taylor asks, breaking me from those happy thoughts.

"We will cordon off that area once we're ready for guests. That was my grandmother's suite, and I still haven't been able to clean out the space. My hope is to eventually consolidate my room and office down that hallway, but that won't likely happen in the next two months."

"I'm sorry. I know that must be difficult, and it's no wonder you've put that area off until last. Take all the time you need."

I give her a tight smile before pushing open the kitchen door. We both stop in our tracks, as we face two strong backs that taper down to tight asses in denim. Taylor's quick squeak draws the men's attention, and they both turn, sleeves rolled up, and soap suds now dripping onto the floor from where they've been washing their hands.

"Gentlemen, you're dripping, not to be confused with drooling," I say with a shake of my head.

They both look down and laugh, turning back toward the sink and fighting over the tap, pushing it back and forth between them, so they can rinse off. I take in Jacob's tight form. I'll never get tired of looking at him. Then Taylor gives a small cough, reminding me she's here. Her eyes flit back and forth between the men, and I can't tell if it's in fear or interest. Her face is implacable, but her eyes are definitely watching. Strands of possessiveness began to creep up my spine with each leftward flit of Taylor's gaze.

"Let me introduce you," I say as Jacob squats down to dry the floor with a rag. "The one who looks good on his knees is Jacob Daniels." Jacob sighs and shakes his head with a chuckle. Garrett barks out a laugh. "And the taller one with the booming laugh is his father, Garrett Daniels. Don't worry, his bark is much worse than his bite." With a grin, I turn back to Taylor. "This is Taylor Wright. She is here about the assistant position, and I'm hoping she takes it."

Taylor stiffens in surprise, and a huge smile spreads across her face as she turns my way. "Really? I mean, thank you! I mean, yes, I'd love to!" She takes a deep breath. "You are serious, right?"

"Of course. Honestly, I knew I wanted to hire you before I gave you the tour, but your ideas and eye for details solidified the decision. These guys here have been helping with the heavy lifting and construction until we are up, running, and making some money, but we'll talk logistics in a bit."

"Nice to meet you, ma'am," Jacob says, extending his hand to shake Taylor's. "I'm here to do whatever it is Morgan needs," He turns his gaze my way and runs his eyes up and down my body. Goosebumps pepper my skin.

Taylor slips her hand from his, catching the hint he's laying on pretty thick. If I hadn't been fighting to not turn 50 shades of pink under his gaze, I'd have laughed. Instead, Mr. Daniels' laughter fills the room again, catching all of our attention.

He's shaking his head. "Get a room, you two."

"We have one, old man, but you need my help cleaning up the mess we made out back."

"Don't get embarrassed in front of your woman and her pixie." He extends his hand to Taylor, though he keeps his eyes on Jacob and me, "The name's Garrett. I can't get Morgan to stop calling me Mr. Daniels, so please don't start. Makes me feel old, and my children do enough of that." When she doesn't respond or take his hand, he looks directly at her. Her brows scrunch together. "Ma'am? Did I say something? Do I stink? I just washed my hands." He holds them up in a placating gesture.

"Pixie?" Taylor asks, raising a brow in the defiant challenge I imagined hiding inside of her. I nearly laugh out loud as his lips draw together and his head tilts in question. "You told Jacob to not embarrass himself in front of Morgan and her pixie. I can only imagine you meant me, and I'd like to know what you meant by it, Mr. Daniels."

When his brows furrow at her use of his proper name, Jacob grabs my hand, pulling me back a step. He might have pulled me to the other room, but there's no way I'm missing this. I need to see how Garrett handles being called out and how Taylor handles his response. I also want to be close enough to step in should this blow way out of proportion. I can only imagine he was talking about her colorful fashion choices, but he might have also meant her youthful appearance. The longer it takes for him to respond, though, the tighter I squeeze Jacob's hand.

"Shit," he says with a chuckle, "I didn't realize I'd said that aloud."

Taylor isn't buying it. She crosses her arms over her chest. "If, at your age, you don't know how not to say the inside thoughts aloud, you should be able to explain them."

"Oh shit," Jacob says so low I'm not sure it hadn't been my own thoughts manifested.

"Ok then, Pixie Girl. If you must know, I took in your colorful self and thought, I bet that's how Tinkerbell would look if she were real and walking around today. And now that I've seen your feistiness, I think I was right."

"Feisty? Tinkerbell? Why, you old cowpoke!"

Jacob and I both step between them. Taylor's face is flushed, but there's no anger in her eyes, and Mr. Daniel's face holds more amusement than anything.

"Mr. Daniels, if you and Jacob would please go finish whatever you were working on, I can finish up with Ms. Wright." As he walks by looking contrite, I whisper, "And if you've scared her off, I'm withdrawing your invitation to the open house."

"I'm so sorry about that," I say, turning back to Taylor.

"They are actually father and son? I would have never guessed his age."

I chuckle at the question. "Ironically, I guessed your age wrong when you first got here, so there must be something in the air. The twins are barely six months older than me, so I can vouch for Garrett's age."

"Twins? Do I even want to know about another tight-assed hunk in that family?"

This time I let out a belly laugh that rivals Garrett's, and it takes several seconds to catch my breath. "Jacob has a twin sister. Joanna's my best friend."

"Best friend's brother, huh?" Taylor asks under her breath, but I catch it and nearly lose myself laughing again.

"Yep, we're a walking small-town romance: best friend's brother, second chance, the one that got away...all the tropes." I chuckle at the joke that practically wrote itself before turning a serious gaze back on Taylor. "I hope we haven't made you change your mind. Mr. Daniels is part of the package, as he's doing work around here, and he's my fiancé's father."

"Oh, he couldn't scare me away, but I might be able to scare him off if you ever want him to be scarce," she responds with a wink, and we both fall into a fit of laughter.

Before Taylor leaves, I want to go over the expectations and needs of the position, the start date, and the gradual increase of hours because I'm starting from nothing. It's embarrassing to ask the woman to take the job without a set schedule and salary, and the possibility she might change her mind because of it has my chest tightening. I hold my breath while Taylor looks over the proposed employment contract.

"Wait, what's this clause mean," Taylor asks, pointing to the last perk I had thought to add as an "if needed" stipulation.

"Oh, I forgot about that because it's in there in case the person who takes the position needs somewhere to stay. Basically, you would have a room here in the house for your use and be able to take meals in the kitchen. There may be times when I might need to be out of town, and my assistant would need to be on hand for guests overnight, so I've included a room in the contract."

Taylor looks up and me with unshed tears.

"Is everything alright?" I ask, walking around the island to put my hand on her shoulder. I want to wrap her in a hug, but I'm not sure it's appropriate. I hadn't expected this type of response to a simple contingency clause.

"Can I hug you?" Taylor asks in response. With a smile, I wrap my arms around her and hold on until she sniffles and pulls away. "I was so worried I would have to say no to the job because of the low hours and pay to start, but a room changes everything. I've been sleeping in my car most nights and only went by a friend's house on the county line to shower this morning before coming here."

The sting of tears burns my eyes at the unexpected confession. "Unfortunately, I cannot start paying you any sooner than outlined here in the contract, but if you would like to start sooner, I can get you a room ready for this evening."

"Really?" she asks on a sob that nearly breaks my heart.

"Yes, now, if you wouldn't mind, I have a few things to do, and I need some things from the Hardware store. Could you go for me?"

"Absolutely," she says, jumping from the stool and grabbing her purse.

I smile at her enthusiasm. "Here, take this for gas. I'll make sure Joanna has everything ready for you, and I'll have a corrected contract printed by the time you return."

When the front door closes tightly behind Taylor, I send a text to Joanna.

> ME: Do you still need a part-time temp to help with inventory and restocking?

JOANNA: Yeah, why?

> ME: Call me.

CHAPTER TWENTY-SIX

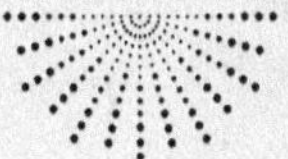

I HAVE TO DO THIS ALONE

Morgan

"I can help if you want. Or I can sit on the floor silently as moral support?"

I don't even turn to look at Taylor whose sympathy is palpable. She doesn't truly understand why I've had such a hard time entering this part of the house and cleaning it out. I tell myself to simply walk down the hall and push the door open, but I just can't do it. Today, though, I'm determined.

"This is something I have to do alone," I say with a big sigh. This is the furthest I've stepped into the hall since Garrett finally got the lock taken off the door. "What do you think about moving the door to the suite to the end of the hall instead of having these separate doors?" The question is a delay tactic, and I can tell Taylor knows it too when she snuffles quietly while trying to hold in a laugh.

"I don't think it's a terrible idea if you want to keep everyone out of that hall completely, but if you want some people to be able to access the business office but not your private rooms, you might want to think about reconfiguring them."

Ugh. She's not wrong, but that's just one more thing to think about and one more thing I don't have money for. Of course, Jacob and Garrett will gladly put in the work to make it happen, but I feel terrible taking advantage of them for non-essential remodeling. It's not that I don't need to move into this suite, because I do. With Taylor using one of the rooms upstairs, and us being completely booked for Spring Break, I have no choice but to move out of the only room I've ever slept in within these walls. I'd just rather sleep on the floor of the basement than in my grandmother's bed, especially with Jacob. We don't need her haunting us and the bed and breakfast.

Taylor takes a step forward at my uncomfortable chuckle, but I hold a hand up to stop her from coming any closer. I have to do this. I can't let my grandmother continue to dictate my life. She's been dead for a long time, and she cost me two decades of happiness already. With that thought in mind, I push open the bedroom door and let the stale air wash over me. There's nothing to fear here. I push out the breath that's been trapped in my lungs and step into the room.

Everything looks exactly like it had months ago when I first walked in here. This time, however, light streams through the windows where I'd left the drapes wide open. When I flip on the light switch, both bedside lamps shine brightly through the space, clearing out all the shadows. My breaths even out and my heart rate settles. I immediately strip the bed, something I should have done the first time I came in here. These linens have been gathering dust for years. The smell of neglect assaults my nostrils as I gather the sheets and comforter and throw them into a heap on the hallway floor.

Next, I pull the roll of trash bags out of my apron pocket and open one. With a sweep of my hand, everything sitting on top of the large dresser goes into the bag. Glass clacks together as the perfume bottles hit bottom. The metal lipstick cases clink against each other before settling amidst the other items. Dust flies everywhere, creating swirls in the rays of sunlight. My grandmother may have been a God-fearing woman with a fire-and-brimstone way about her, but she insisted on looking and smelling good. She'd be livid to see the dust particles floating around and blanketing all her belongings. I smile out of sheer spite.

27
EPILOGUE

*J*acob

"Boy, if you don't get your ass out here, you're gonna be late to your own damn wedding!"

Jesus Christ, this old man is really going to make me choke him. I told Morgan it was a bad idea for me to come back home the night before the ceremony, but she had insisted. Now, I have to deal with Pa's bullshit rushing me. As if it isn't enough that he's the one walking my wife down the aisle. *My wife.* My breaths stutter at the word. Morgan is about to finally be my fucking wife. I swallow the emotion and respond with the most sarcasm possible.

"Just because your girlfriend is already at the house doesn't mean you have to give me shit."

Rather than respond with something scathing, Pa chuckles from the other side of the door. That laugh almost infuriates me more. I'm here holding back tears, and he's out there laughing. I yank open the door, ready to let out all my frustrations on him, but he's standing right there like a statue. Surprise has me rearing backwards, nearly tripping over the bag behind me.

Reaching out to grab my shoulders, Pa holds me steady. When

I get my balance and look up into his eyes, they're filled with unshed tears, and my own dam breaks. He wraps me in his arms like he used to years ago, and I hold him back, my arms around his waist.

"I'm so happy for you, Jacob. You found the love of your life, and though you couldn't hold her physically for years, you held her in your heart until she made her way back. Your mother would be so proud." The last bit came out on a shuddering breath, and I matched it with a sob.

"I wish she were here to see this. She always loved Morgan."

"She's watching, son. She's watching, and she's happy for you both."

He holds me for a few moments longer before clapping my back a couple times and stepping away. I square my shoulders and wipe the tears from my face. Once my emotions are back in check, I nod to him and pick up the overnight bag that nearly ended my life earlier.

"Let's go get me married."

Pa claps my shoulder, letting out a hearty laugh. "Yeah, let's go do that."

*M*organ

I worry my bottom lip. Jacob and Garrett haven't left the farm yet. Taylor has been giving me updates between each of the wedding-planner tasks she's taken on over the past few weeks once it got to be too much for me.

"Stop eating off your lipstick, Morgan," Joanna reprimands. "There's no reason to be nervous. I don't know shit about shit, but the one thing I do know is that my brother will burn down all of Cole County to get here in time to marry you."

I laugh, but tears sting my eyes. She's right about Jacob. He will be here, and we will be married today. Finally. Of that, I have no doubt. But the wedding isn't the only thing at stake today. I don't get a chance to tell Joanna that, though, as Taylor yells down the hall that guests have started arriving. Suddenly, the room is a flurry of movement as my wedding party, as tiny as it is, puts the final touches on their looks and reapply any makeup that's worn off or smudged.

"We're here," a deep and soothing voice says from the doorway. A gasp sounds from behind me, but I'm not sure which of the two women make the sound.

"Thank you, Mr. Daniels," I say, turning to smile at the older man whose face so resembles the one I plan to wake up to every morning for as long as he can stand me.

"Are you ready, Morgan? I'm not sure my son will be able to stand outside for very long before he storms through the door to make sure you haven't run out."

Laughter bubbles out of me. I can absolutely picture Jacob crashing through the wall like the Kool-Aid man and hauling me over his shoulder. Garrett smiles and holds out his arm for me. I take one last look at the full-length mirror behind me. It's one of the only things I kept from my grandmother. When I focus hard on my face, I can almost see her and my mother staring back. Their choices might have made my life more difficult, but they eventually brought me back home at the right time. Now, I get to choose happiness over everything.

"Ready," I say and place my hand in the crook of his elbow.

I had wanted to exit the house through the back porch, but Taylor insisted that we walk around the house, so Jacob would get his first look at all of me, and not just the parts that showed through the screened-in openings. Lucky for her, it isn't raining, else we might've scrapped the whole plan and just said our vows in the dining room. She's already in her feelings because Garrett is walking me down the aisle instead of her. Jacob's best friend Trevor is serving as her escort for the ceremony because Joanna begged me to let her boyfriend stand on Jacob's side, just so he could hold her hand the entire way. If one more thing was to change, I believe Taylor's eyes really would pop out of her head.

Taylor's dramatic antics don't matter, though, because when the music changes, and everyone turns tear-filled eyes toward me, the only person I can see is Jacob. His smile is electrifying, and it steadies me. That smile tells me there is nothing that will make him change his mind, and when he takes my hands after Garrett releases me, I lean into him for a kiss.

"Get a room," Joanna hisses from behind me, and the entire wedding party chuckles under their breath.

"I hate you," I whisper in her direction, making sure that the other guests can't read my lips, and she simply shrugs.

There aren't many people here, which is exactly the way we want it. Jacob and Joanna are the only real friends I've ever had until Taylor. Now, I've added her best friend Jordan to my retinue. She's the one who lovingly designed my gown to not only fit my curves perfectly but also my personality. It's so perfect, I nearly cried when I first tried it on. Since her brother is Joanna's boyfriend, I also invited their parents. Jacob has a few more friends than me, having lived his whole life in this one town, but there are still very few he'd wanted with us here today.

"Let's get through the ceremony before we get to the loving and the arguing," says a voice coming from my left.

When I turn to face Wilber Crawley, I can't help but smile. He and his wife finish out our little gathering, and I'm so grateful they're here. Jordan introduced me to Ruth Crawley at their family diner a few months back when she took me, Joanna, and Taylor on a recognizance mission to try on different wedding dresses and find what I liked and what I didn't. Though I spent most of my life moving around to different parts of Cole County with my mother, I never felt a part of the county. Apparently, the Crawley's are pillars of the community, so when Ruth found out

I'd been in the area my whole life but hadn't heard of her husband, she wanted to know how.

Rather than going into details, I talked about Jacob and me. She was so moved by our second-chance romance that she offered to make our wedding cake. No, offered isn't quite the right word. She insisted. I didn't have the heart to tell her I'd planned to make it myself. As we finished up our lunch that day, Old Man Wilber, as Joanna affectionately called him, walked in. Ruth recounted the story to him, and he, in turn, insisted on officiating today's ceremony. We hadn't even thought about who would preside over our vows to each other, and, much like his wife, Wilber wouldn't take no for an answer.

Thus, begins the wedding ceremony, unorthodox like the rest of our relationship has been, with strangers turned friends. Jacob recites his vows first, following all the traditional promises. With each word, butterflies take flight in my stomach, and by the time he says, "I do," my palms are sweating, and breakfast is threatening to make a reappearance. I swallow the nerves along with the tears and pull out a slip of paper from the hidden pocket I'd insisted Jordan sew into my gown.

"If it's alright," I say as Wilber turns his attention to me, "I have something I'd like to read."

Wilber nods. Jacob's grip on my hands tightens, and when I look up into his eyes, there's a mixture of love, confusion, and a hint of fear. We hadn't talked about writing our own vows. In truth, we hadn't thought much about the ceremony itself at all. After all this time, we had already made our promises to each other in all the ways that mattered to us. Today was a formality. A trip into the city yesterday, though, had me thinking about these vows and compelled me to write my own. With a smile that I hope conveys all the love I have for this man, I unfold the piece of paper and begin reading:

Twenty-five years ago, my life was a war zone, and the only reprieve was knowing I'd be taken to Colliers Town every summer where my two best friends, my only two friends, lived. Something happened over the next four years or so. Something shifted, and what had been nothing more than friendly affection morphed into puppy love. Then, as brotherly hair pulling shifted to pinky promises, real love took over. How ironic that it all came to an end with our first kiss as infatuated teens, and now we get ready to start the love story we'd had written in the stars with a new kiss, our first kiss as husband and wife. I never believed I deserved you, but you waited on me. I never understood what you saw in me, yet you still waited. I don't know that I'll ever feel worthy of your patience, but what I do know is that I'll never make you wait again. So, take these words as my vow to you:

I promise to love and appreciate you for all that you are until my last breath and far beyond forever.
I promise to stand secure in our love and the life that we build together until my last breath and beyond.
I promise to never let a day go by where you don't know the depth of my love, whether I'm breathing or not.
And I promise that this new life we're bringing into the world will know that our love transcends time and space from the moment they draw breath until forever.

Before I finish the words, Jacob drops to his knees, and a collective gasp sounds across the people gathered. I kneel in front of him and take his face in my hands. His eyes are closed, and tears have collected along his lashes. I kiss each eye, tasting the saltiness of his emotions. When he opens his eyes, there is a single question written in his gaze, and I nod. His hands find my waist and slide around to the front of my belly where the once soft and squishy skin has barely begun to tighten into a bump.

"How'd I not know?" he asks quietly, shock evident in his voice.

"I didn't know until yesterday, not for sure anyway."

He looks up at me with awe, and the knot that's been in my throat since the doctor's visit yesterday releases. Tears well in my eyes when one of his hands grabs the back of my neck and pulls me close enough to rest our forehead together. I take in a shuddering breath.

"Are you upset I didn't tell you yesterday?" I ask when he doesn't say anything.

His mouth opens and closes several times before he just shakes his head and covers my mouth with his. Wrapping his other arm around my waist, he pulls us both up on our knees until our bodies are pressed together. The kiss is long, passionate, and wet with our tears.

"Well, ladies and gents," Wilber says from where he towers above us, "I do believe he has kissed the bride. We'll let them worry about the rings later."

A cheer rings out as everyone starts clapping, but I can't care less. Here, in Jacob's arms, is where I've always belonged and where I plan to stay, rings on our fingers or in our pockets, or hidden in the bottom of a closet. This man and this love we share is all I'll ever need.

LEYA LAYNE

Leya Layne's love of a Happily Ever After started with Disney. Then she found romance novels in her early teens thanks to a bag of Harlequin novels hidden under her grandmother's dresser. She got her HEA fix for the rest of her teen years thanks to a well-worn library card. Though she is currently publishing contemporary romances that have been described as Hot Hallmark, don't be surprised to see her delve into historical or paranormal in the future. The possibilities are endless, but the one thing she'll promise is that they'll all be spicy!

Follow Leya all over social media:
https://linktr.ee/LeyaLayneAuthor

See her website for forthcoming releases and trigger/content warnings:
https://bisabelwrites.com/leyas-content-is-for-18-only/

Coming Soon

December 2025: Magnolia Cove: A Cozy Romance Anthology

February 2025: Whiskey Falls Anthology

April 2025: Elinora

You've Got Bookmail

Shar's Story

Love with a Vengeance

Carol's Christmas Awakening

Clarissa and the Wallflower

Breadcrumbs

Josefina

Cole County Anthology Series (Unpublished Dec 31, 2025)

Something Old (Magnolia Cove Anthology Book 1)

Coming in 2026

Living for You

Yearning for You

Trying for You

Reaching for You

Elinora

Raquel

Whiskey Falls (The Distilleries Anthology Book 1)

Fireproof

#JustRight (If I'm really feeling froggy…if not, 2027)